Lock Down Publications and Ca$h
Presents

I0637449

STEPPERS 3

The Richest Opp

Written By

King Rio

First Edition 2024

Printed in the United States of America

Lock Down Publications
P.O. Box 944
Stockbridge, GA 30281
www.lockdownpublications.com

Like our page on Facebook: Lock Down Publications
www.facebook.com/lockdownpublications.ldp

Stay Connected with Us!

Text **LOCKDOWN** to 22828 to stay up-to-date with new releases, sneak peaks, contests and more...

Like our page on Facebook:
Lock Down Publications

Join Lock Down Publications/The New Era Reading Group

Visit our website:
www.lockdownpublications.com

Follow us on Instagram:
Lock Down Publications

Email Us: We want to hear from you!

PROLOGUE

"Y'all see it," the man on Bam's phone screen said, pointing a gold-plated fifty-caliber Desert Eagle at the neatly stacked mountain of hundred-dollar bills on the glass-top cocktail table in front of him. "That's $5 million. If one of y'all want it, all you gotta do is find that nigga, Lejon White, and put him in the dirt."

Bam's eyes got big, and it wasn't necessarily because of the cash amount. Five million dollars wasn't really a whole lot of money to him. Bam was the CEO of a successful club and concert promoting business, but lowkey he was a certified drug kingpin. The last load of drugs he'd purchased from his connect had included two hundred kilos of cocaine, a hundred kilos of heroin, seventy kilos of fentanyl, and a thousand pounds of exotic marijuana. He had $19 million in legitimate income in his bank account, another $34 million stashed in safes at eight different properties, and he usually kept at least $500,000 in cash in a Louis Vuitton duffle bag in the back of his blacked-out Rolls Royce Cullinan.

His eyes got big not because he was stunned by the large sum of cash that was on the cocktail table but because he'd never heard of anyone offering that much for a murder. But from Johnny "Bang Boy" Broward, older brother to billionaire Panteon Tech CEO Johnna Broward, it was only to be expected.

One of the four black suited men seated on the black leather sofa with Bang Boy got up and ended the video call, and Bam turned to look at the man Bang Boy had put the five million dollar hit on. There were five of them standing around the massive living room of the Highland Park mansion that Lejon "Grizzy" White and his wife, Nya, had moved into just three days ago. They were Bam, Grizzy, Nya, Grizzy's cousin, Marcus, and Nya's best friend, Lacey. The mansion was owned by Blake "Bulletface" King, the Grammy-winning rap artist and billionaire CEO of Money Bagz Management, one of the leading record labels in the music industry. Nya had signed with MBM just six days ago, and already she had a single featuring Bulletface that was heating up the airwaves nationwide. It was called *Step So Hard*, and in her two verses, Nya gave vague references to the slew of homicides she and Grizzy were suspected of committing over the past few months. The song was a banger. Bam had listened to it on the ride over.

Right now though, the rapper known as Young Nya didn't look all that excited about her flourishing music career. In fact, she looked downright worried.

"This hoe ass nigga done dropped a bag on somebody while he ducked off way out in California somewhere," she muttered discontentedly.

Grizzy said nothing, but Bam could see the muscles in his jaws repeatedly flexing as he clenched and unclenched his teeth and stared into his Styrofoam cup of iced Sprite soda and Wockhardt syrup. He was a big man — six three, maybe two sixty, all muscle — clad in a skin hugging Gucci wife beater over shorts and sneakers. His pockets were stuffed full of cash. His white diamond, infinity link necklace had a diamond flooded pendant hanging from it that depicted a grizzly chomping down on his nickname, and his bracelet matched the necklace.

The others were dressed just as gaudily, but what really caught Bam's eyes were weapons. Every one of them had a 7.62-millimeter mini-Draco pistol clutched in one hand or the other, and each Draco had either a fifty round banana clip or a high-capacity drum magazine. As a high-ranking gang leader, Bam was carrying such powerful weapons, but he hadn't seen women toting them.

And Nya looked like she was itching to use hers.

"Johnna behind this shit," Grizzy said after a time. "She knew what Bang Boy was on when she hugged me at the strip club last week. I saw it in her eyes. The way she was actin'. She knew he had just got my pops killed in the feds, and she knew Bang Boy was comin' home from the feds that upcoming Monday, and she ain't say shit about that either."

"I'd say she more than knew about it," said Lacey, the 6'2" Amazon of a woman who rarely went anywhere without Nya by her side. "That hoe played a part in this shit. She's mad that you made her pay back all that money she stole."

Lacey was like a giant standing next to Nya, who stood just 4'10" and was maybe a hundred and ten pounds, but it was clear from the way everyone kept looking at her that she was at the top of the hierarchy within their tight knit circle.

Bam's deceased brother had dated Nya for a short while last year. He'd brought her through the north Lawndale neighborhood almost every day, showing her off in the passenger's seat of his drop top Impala. Back then, Nya had seemed like such a sweet, little, bad bitch. It wasn't until recently that Bam had started hearing all the war stories about her — that she had hopped out on Sleet, the then leader of the Cold Gang faction of Conservative Vice Lords and gunned him down on his front porch with a modified Glock that spit out rounds like a machine gun. Minutes later, a member of the Wicked Town faction of Traveling Vice Lords named Crunchy was driving a stolen car through his neighborhood when a short, redbone, who looked a lot like Nya, hopped out of a Trackhawk and shot him with a Draco. And then, just a few weeks ago, a member of the Angelo faction of Four Corner Hustlers had tried to carjack Grizzy for his blue Corvette and didn't see Nya standing there on the passenger's side. The attempted carjacker had caught a valley of bullets to the face, and one of the gang members who tried coming to his aid had been gunned down with him. Since then, Nya had become somewhat of a legend on the streets of Chicago, and she'd further cemented her legacy when she showed up at Redbone's Gentlemen's Club the weekend before last and posted up with her girls in the VIP section, just a few tables over from Crunchy's brother, Curry, Wobble, the chief of the Wicked Town TVLs, and Frenchy, the man who'd replaced Sleet as the new chief of the Cold Gang CVLs. Nya and her all-female crew — they had recently started calling themselves Plush Gang on social media — hadn't waited long before they kicked off the violence. When Curry's girlfriend, Lyric, got up to go to the restroom, they'd jumped her right then and there, beating her with their fists, their high heeled shoes, and half empty Cosamigos bottles, and then, they'd done the same thing to Curry while Grizzy and Marcus easily defeated Wobble, Frenchy, and several others.

Video of the epic brawl had quickly gone viral, mainly because Curry, Frenchy, and Wobble had been shot and killed once they walked out of the strip club and also because it was Nya who'd kicked off the fight.

"I don't really care if Johnna was involved or not," Nya said, fingering the diamond MBM pendant attached to her diamond cuban link necklace. "If Bang Boy's in it, Johnna's in it too. And if Johnna's in it, her lil sisters, Johnesha and Johnetta, are on my shit list right along with her."

"They're all at Rick Rubin's all-white party in The Hamptons," Lacey said, holding up her iPhone so everyone could see it. "This is video of Beyoncé and JayZ at the party, but you can see Johnna and her sisters in the background."

"Forget about them for now." Nya set her mini-Draco on one of the ottomans and pulled out her own iPhone. "Johnesha owns that Mercedes Benz dealership in Streeterville. Her boyfriend, Lamont, runs it. I'll pop right out on his ass."

7

"Whatever you do," Bam said, looking at Grizzy, "I wouldn't advise leaving this mansion for a while. Especially not today. It's the Fourth of July. Too many guns and fireworks going off. You got five Ms on yo head, bruh, and he just gang offered that to me and six other gang leaders. That's a whole lotta money."

"Fuck all them niggas. I got millions too," Grizzy replied. But he didn't sound all that convincing.

Chapter 1

Bam sent a screenshot to Grizzy's phone before he left. It showed the faces of all seven leaders who'd been on the FaceTime call with Bang Boy, and one of them immediately caught Grizzy's eye.

Roberto "Viejo" Ortega was the regional inca for the Latin Kings in the "Crown Town" neighborhood, which essentially meant he was the top Latin King for every section, or chapter, in the area. Grizzy had met him at a White Sox game about ten years ago, back when Grizzy and Marcus were heavy into robbing drug dealers, and within a week, they had talked Viejo into having one of his female runners deliver four kilos of cocaine to them in a rival Black Disciple neighborhood. They'd robbed the girl for the four bricks of coke and laughed about it when the Latin Kings returned and killed two BDs on 61st and King Drive. Viejo had wanted them dead ever since.

Grizzy was familiar with three others in the screenshot. Baby Stone was a general for the Black P. Stones from somewhere out west. He'd done time with Grizzy at Menard Correctional Center in the early 2000s. Murder was the highest-ranking Black Disciple in the city of Chicago, and Boanie Black was the leader of the Black Gangster New Breeds. Nya and Lacey pointed out that Bryce, the leader of the Cold Gang CVLs, was another face in the screenshot. Grizzy had dumped him on his face during the strip club brawl two Fridays ago, but he hadn't really gotten a good

9

look at the short, light skinned man until now. Grizzy and his gang had already been trying to track down Bryce's younger cousin, Jabar, who'd briefly dated Grizzy's nineteen-year-old daughter, Kamari, in a failed effort to obtain Grizzy's home address. As soon as Grizzy figured out where Bryce and Jabar were hiding out, he was going to kill them. Simple as that.

The four of them — Nya, Lacey, Marcus, and Grizzy — were seated in the spacious living room of what used to be the Michael Jordan mansion. It was 10:00 p.m. on Independence Day, and the sound of fireworks exploding nearby had Grizzy on edge. He took a large swallow from his narcotic beverage, went to Johnna Broward's Instagram page, and watched video of her and her sisters mingling with celebrities at Rick Rubin's enormous glass mansion in The Hamptons.

"I ain't gon' lie," Nya said. "This shit done blew my whole night. I bet not never see that nigga, Bang Boy, in traffic. On my grandma grave."

Marcus only shook his head. He was leaning forward, breaking up buds of exotic marijuana on the front of a *Kite* magazine with Lil Durk on the cover. Lacey was rolling a blunt too. Glancing at the two of them, Grizzy thought of the video Lacey had posted to Instagram last week. It had shown her and Marcus lying out by an infinity pool behind a mansion they had rented from AirBnB, and at the end of the video, Marcus could be heard off camera saying that Grizzy and Nya should have given them more than $50,000 apiece out of the $23 million Johnna had wired to Grizzy's bank account.

Grizzy had folded after that. Marcus and Lacey had been down from the start, and Nya agreed that rewarding them with a lousy $50,000 was plain wrong, so Grizzy had sent Marcus an additional $700,000, and Nya had sent Lacey another $200,000. They'd also let the couple move into the mansion with them, and Grizzy had given Marcus his triple black Jeep Grand Cherokee Trailhawk. Neither Marcus nor Lacey had complained about their share of the money ever since.

But now, there was $5 million on Grizzy's head, and he found himself wondering if that was enough of an incentive to turn his cousin against him.

He got up and left the living room without a word. Nya was seconds behind him. He knew it because he could hear the steady click of her Bottega heels on the white, marble floor. She was wearing a ruffled, gray, Gucci top and designer jeans that looked like Edward Scissorhands had gotten ahold of them. Her fingernails were like claws and impeccably manicured with a glittery silver finish. She'd had her long, dark hair colored blond, like the wigs Lacey always wore, and it was parted straight up the middle.

"Can you believe we're actually staying in a mansion that Alexus and Bulletface used to live in?" Nya said in wavering tones of amazement. When Grizzy didn't respond, her tone softened, and she added, "We can forget that club appearance. I'll just text Quita and Niecy and tell them to go on without us. I'll call Streets over and get back in the booth. Record a few more songs."

"Nah, we still goin," Grizzy said, tilting his Draco up onto his shoulder. "I'm just gon' have the folks slide with us from now on. They gone pull up twenty deep. On Harry Hoover, ain't a nigga on Earth tough enough to keep me in the house. Like Mo3 said, we steppin' night and day. Fuck Bang Boy."

Nya laughed as she ran around in front of him. She turned and started walking backwards, biting down on her bottom lip and smiling around her perfect, white squares of teeth.

"They can't fuck with us, baby," she said, cradling her mini-Draco against her belly. "I mean, think about it. Every nigga that done crossed us done got hit up. Sleet. Crunchy. Frenchy. Wobble. Mikey and Derrick. Them niggas who shot up my daddy. Them four lil niggas who tried to jump you in VIP. The goofy who tried to carjack us. We dropped so many bodies that Bryce tried to call and cop deuces." She threw back her head and laughed merrily as she spun around and continued walking forward. "Fuck the opps. They done fucked up now anyway and gave me a record deal. I ain't never gone let up off they necks. It's up there. And Bang Boy gone be the next one to get his head knocked off."

Grizzy's mouth spread into an amused grin. He licked his lips and stared down at Nya's ass. It was getting fatter, filling out. She was a badass, little redbone like Moneybagg Yo's girlfriend, Ari. And pretty soon, she would be a superstar. In fact, she'd passed up on the opportunity to join Alexus, Bulletface, and several artists at Rick Rubin's exclusive A-list party just to hang out with her husband, her Plush Gang clique, and Grizzy's "Deg Pound" faction of Gangster Disciples at her very first paid nightclub appearance. Bankroll Reese, the owner of The Visionary Lounge, had offered Nya $50,000 to turn up in VIP and another $50,000 if she performed her new hit single, and she'd happily accepted both offers.

Just looking at her made Grizzy's dick twitch in his shorts. As soon as they entered the master bedroom, he closed and locked the door and set his Draco on the California king bed. Nya tossed hers right next to his, turned on the playlist of unreleased songs she'd recorded over the past week or so, and started twerking with her tongue out and her hands on her knees.

"I got my first paid show, ayyy, ayyy, ayyy!" Nya said cheerfully.

Grizzy cracked up laughing and slapped his hands onto her hips. He picked her up and placed her on the bed. She twerked on her hands and knees, winding her hips, looking back at him.

It was the sexiest shit he'd ever seen in his life.

"What time you gotta be at that club?" Grizzy asked, gripping her waistline and snatching her back against the front of his shorts.

"Fifteen minutes before midnight."

Grizzy looked at his diamond-flooded Rolex Sky-Dweller. It told him the time was 10:08 p.m.

"Aw, we got plenty of time," he said, flipping her over and undoing her Chanel belt buckle.

Chapter 2

The seventh man in the FaceTime screenshot was Dwayne Kelly, a five-star universal elite for the Undertaker Vice Lords who went by the name U.T.

He was a fat man, though not morbidly. He ate a lot of food and took a lot of shits, and when it came to the Cicero Avenue area on Chicago's west side, he lorded over it like Vladimir Putin, ordering his foot soldiers to murder anyone opposing him. Instead of missiles and drones, his army used Glocks and assault rifles, and though there was no oil to sell, there was plenty of heroin.

He was in the backseat of his black Jeep Grand Wagoneer during the video call, being tailed by two carloads of armed security. He'd practically salivated looking at the mountain of cash on Bang Boy's cocktail table. U.T. was up a few hundred grand, and his two heroin spots were doing numbers, but he'd been taking losses left and right.

Over the past four months, he'd had to pay for five different funerals. Three of them were younger Undertakers who'd died by the gun. The other two were his blood relatives — his eighty-one-year-old aunt, Bessie, who'd passed in her sleep, and his cousin, Sleet, who'd been shot and killed in front of his west side home, allegedly by the wife of the man whose head Bang Boy had just dropped $5 million on, and to make matters worse, the DEA had raided one of his trap houses and a stash house just five days ago. They'd arrested eight of his dealers and seized twenty-two guns, twelve Glock switches, two kilos of heroin, four hundred grams of fentanyl, and over $92,000 in cash. He needed that $5 million like a flat bootied stripper needed a Brazilian butt lift.

Which was why he had spent just a couple of minutes at his daughter's backyard barbecue before climbing back into his full-size SUV and telling his girlfriend, Shameika, to drive him to the Courtway Building on Congress and Cicero. He sent a text message to Carmen "The Prince" Richardson, another high-ranking Undertaker, and had him organize an emergency gang meeting at the apartment building. By the time he walked through the door of Apartment 5E, there was a circle of fifteen young gangsters standing in the living room with their right hands clasped tightly around the backs of their left wrists, just above their waistlines. It was the Vice Lord stance.

U.T. took his position in the circle of men and spoke.

"We got a lick, Lords," he began. "I'm talkin' about a *life* changer. The kinda lick that'll set a nigga straight for *life*." He paused for dramatic effects then yanked his pants up by the belt loop and sailed on. "I just got off the phone with one of the Moes from out south. The man offered me a million dollars cash to get a nigga knocked off."

"Man, where he at?" It was thirty-year-old Puncho, the five-star branch elite for the Undertakers who'd been assigned the position of chief enforcer over four years ago. Tall, dark, and impossibly ugly with dreads that were rough and tangled at the roots. he was the man U.T. had put in charge of carrying out physical violations when other members broke the rules. "I'll take care of that asap. Just tell me where to find him."

"If I knew where to find him, I'd do it myself," U.T. said tightly. "All we need is video of buddy getting whacked. We get that, we got the money, and I'll split it with whoever handle that business. His name Lejon White, but they call him Grizzy. He a GD from 72nd and Green. They say he just married Nya, that new lil rap chick."

Several sets of eyebrows went up. There wasn't a gang member in the city of Chicago who hadn't heard of Nya Mixon, and it had nothing to do with her new hit song. It was her reputation. She'd stepped on some real factors, and she was blatantly arrogant about it. She uploaded photos to social media with massive stacks of hundreds held up to her ear. She always had a crew of bitches with her, and it was a known fact that if you tried her, your chances of living to see another day were slim to none.

"She can get stretched too," said Tyrin, a teenaged Undertaker who, in the last six months, had committed four homicides and an equal number of armed robberies under U.T.'s orders. He was just under six feet tall, a slim, light skinned, handsome eighteen-year-old with tattoos from neck to waist. "She used to stay over there on Central. Her and that tall bitch. We need to slide through there."

"Nah, she in a mansion now," Puncho said. "Look at her Instagram. She just signed with MBM. She got a song with Bulletface. Shorty got a bag now. It's gon be hard to catch up with them."

There were a few other suggestions, none of them of any real value. And then, Puncho's eyes widened very suddenly, and he took out his phone and started typing. U.T. watched him closely; the others broke up the circle, some of them strategizing, others lurking on Nya's Instagram page, but U.T's unwavering gaze remained locked on Puncho.

"What's the thought, Lord ?" U.T. asked, crossing the room to stand next to his enforcer. "What's on yo mind?"

"I know somebody who can get us close to Grizzy," Puncho said.

Forty-eight-year-old Dwayne " U.T." Kelly stared down at the text message Puncho was typing on his smartphone. He smiled after he read it and patted the ruthless younger man on the shoulder.

"Good thinkin'," U.T. said, smiling and nodding his head contentedly as he listened to the distant boom of fireworks. He was seeing dollar signs.

Chapter 3

Nya loved sitting on Grizzy's face, and judging from the way he held on to her thighs and sucked on her clitoris as she rocked back and forth on his mouth, he loved it just as much as she did.

Alexus and Bulletface must have enjoyed watching themselves in the bedroom because there were mirrors everywhere. On the ceiling. On the walls. On the doors. Everywhere Nya looked, she saw herself riding Grizzy's face, her titties bouncing and jiggling as she did it.

She'd taken off all her clothes, but she still wore all her jewelry. She liked the way the light refracted off the flawless white diamonds, creating awe inspiring rainbow colors every time she moved. The ice in her Chanel hoop earrings and Rolex watch hit the same way. Just knowing that they had millions of dollars in their joint bank account (Johnna Broward had sent Grizzy the $23 million she'd stolen from his father, and Nya had received a $950,000 signing bonus from Bulletface to sign with Money Bagz Management) had Nya in a blissful state of mind, and that combined with the intense feel of Grizzy's fervently sucking mouth, it was a moment she hoped would last forever.

She looked down at Grizzy's face and ran her fingertips over the waves in his hair. He was such a handsome man. And he was thirty-seven, a full sixteen years older than she was, which, for several reasons, made her love him even more. He had morals and values. His priorities were in perfect order. He knew how to take care of and, at the same time, put his woman first. Their dates consisted of relaxing visits to upscale massage parlors, dinner at five-star restaurants, and bomb sex in five-thousand-dollar penthouse suites. He'd taken Nya to the Bahamas for her birthday week, and he'd surprised her with another diamond watch — a $140,000 Audemars Piguet — and a second Hermes Birkin bag to celebrate her record deal.

Lejon White was the husband of her dreams.

Nya inhaled deeply, and her body trembled. She dropped her head back and gawked at her open-mouthed expression in the ceiling mirror. She watched herself freeze up as the orgasm hit her like a stun gun.

Grizzy licked and slurped the orgasmic juices out of her as she came. When the aftershocks passed, she tumbled off of him and lay flat on her stomach, momentarily exhausted from the orgasm, but he gave her no time to recover. He slipped an arm under her belly, lifted her onto her knees, and eased his fat, ten-inch erection into her dripping pussy.

For a while, Nya lay on the side of her face with her mouth wide open, her mind vacant, her lashy eyes agape. A falsetto of high-pitched moans escaped her throat sporadically. Grizzy went in deep, and she tried to crawl forward, tried to run from it, but Grizzy's hands were like vise grips.

"Where the fuck you think you goin?" Grizzy asked. "Hm? Where you goin? Where you runnin' to?"

Nya gave no answer. She balled the plush, white, goose-down comforter into her fists and squeezed. She moaned some more — loud, screaming moans — then experienced a fleeting moment of relief when Grizzy pulled out and smacked his rock-hard phallus off her ass. He spread open her butt cheeks, spit on her asshole, and penetrated the tight, little hole with his thumb as his fat, black snake slithered back into her.

She came again. It was a more intense orgasm than the first one. Grizzy kept fucking her, holding her waist and slamming his dick in and out of her for another minute or so, and then, he shoved in deep and growled through clenched teeth as he spilled his seed inside of her.

They lay panting for several moments afterward, Nya on her stomach, Grizzy on his back. Nya laughed after a time. Then, she reached over and poked the pointed tip of one fingernail into his jaw.

"You sure yo ain't tryna collect one of those bounties they got on my head? 'Cause I feel like you just tried to murder me," she said.

Grizzy's deep, throaty chuckle brought a glorious smile to Nya's face. "I ain't gon' lie," he said, running one hand up and down the six sharply defined bricks of his abdomen. "That five million got me nervous."

"Well, let's put the same amount on him."

"That ain't gon' do shit. He way out in California. His sister worth thirteen, fourteen billion. We can't compete with that. And five Ms on a nigga head in the 'Raq is a guaranteed death sentence. Niggas kill their own mama for that kinda money, and Bang Boy just made that offer to seven gang *leaders*."

"We can move to Atlanta," Nya said, rolling out of bed. "Or Los Angeles. Or Miami. We ain't gotta stay here in the city. We can go to war with these niggas from a thousand miles away."

Grizzy went silent. Nya went to the bathroom to freshen up, and he joined her a minute later. Now, the palpable threat of Bang Boy's five-million-dollar bounty consumed her thoughts entirely. There were other things in the back of her mind — Bulletface had a private jet scheduled to transport her and her entourage to Miami at 2:00 a.m., about fifty of her favorite Hip Hop celebrities had recently followed her on Instagram, along with three hundred thousand others, bringing her follower count up to 620,000, Bulletface had thirty-two exotic cars parked in the underground garage, and he'd given Nya permission to drive any one she chose — but there was nothing more important than her and her husband's safety.

"Who does he run with?" Nya asked a few minutes later as she sat in front of a mirror in the massive two-story, walk-in closet where she stored her dozens of pairs of designer shoes and handbags. "Bang Boy, I mean. He has to run with somebody in the city. He had four other niggas with him. What's their names?"

Grizzy shrugged his shoulders. He was brushing his hair at a closet mirror behind her. He wore Balaclavas and sunglasses. "I think Mondré was one of 'em. He was Bang Boy's right-hand man back in the day. I shot Montré in the back wit' an AK on 71st and Rhodes back in oh-two. Another one of them niggas might've been Butter. He used to be with Bang Boy all the time. I can't really tell if he was on the couch from that screenshot."

Touching up her makeup, Nya tried to come up with a plan. Seven gang leaders knew that there was $5 million being offered for her husband's murder. Grizzy would be traveling with her to Miami in just a few hours. Maybe she'd be able to talk him into staying there for a couple of weeks, or maybe months. They could put $50,000 on each of Bang Boy's close friends and wait it out, let the streets take care of them.

"Aren't you even a lil worried about Bam?" Nya asked. "He knows you're here. And he is one of the seven gang leaders Bang Boy offered that money to."

Grizzy shook his head. "I spend too much money with him. I just had Smoke grab ten bricks of boy from that nigga. That was $600,000. He ain't gon' fuck me over."

$5 million is a lot more than $600,000, Nya thought, but she kept her opinion to herself as she stood up and turned around to face Grizzy. She'd changed into a sexy, see-through, Balenciaga dress with a black Savage X Fenty bra

and thong panties underneath it. She dug in her black croc skin Birkin bag, pulled out her phone, went to the camera, and snapped about twenty photos standing at the closet mirror with Grizzy right behind her.

"If you post one of them pictures," Grizzy said, "don't mention we're on our way to The Visionary Lounge."

"Shit." Nya paused to think it over then, "I'll just put some emojis with it. Something simple."

She was swiping through the photos, trying to decide which one to post, when Grizzy said, "I know you're pregnant."

"Huh?" Nya looked up from her phone, a smirk playing at the corners of her mouth as she eyed his reflection. "What are you talking about?"

"You stopped smokin' and drinkin' after we went to that strip club last week." He pointed out. "Plus, Lacey told Marcus about you missin' your period. I just didn't say nothin'. Was waitin' on you to bring it up."

Nya turned around to look up at him again, full out smiling now. He put his arm around her and grabbed her ass. She pursed her lips for a kiss, and he gave it to her without a moment's hesitation, but it wasn't the passionate kiss she'd been hoping for. It was a cold, rough kiss, delivered with an equally frigid expression.

"I know about Quendell too," Grizzy said. The palm of his right hand came down hard on her left buttock. It stung and made her jump a little "You're my *wife*, Nya. We're *married*. Stop fuckin' keepin' secrets from me."

She sighed and lowered her head against his chest. Quendell "Q" Hardiman was her four-year-old son from a previous relationship. The brilliant little boy was in her mother's custody. They were with her father, Goldie, in Mesa, Arizona, living in a two-bedroom apartment Nya was paying for until they could find a nice house she could buy for them. Nya had wanted to tell Grizzy about Q, but she hadn't been willing to admit that she'd given up custody of her son, so she could run the streets with her friends. Lacey had a daughter the same age as Q, and she'd done the same thing Nya had done, handing little Sparkle over to her mother, so she wouldn't have to put up with raising her. But while Nya was still in denial, Lacey had already begun bringing her daughter around. The inquisitive little girl had visited the mansion twice already. Lacey and Marcus had taken Sparkle and three of Marcus' kids to see the fireworks at Navy Pier a few hours ago.

"I'm sorry, Lejon," Nya murmured, really meaning it.

"We'll talk about it later," Grizzy said. He gave her another slap on the ass, a much lighter slap than before. "Come on. Let's get to that bag."

Chapter 4

There were three blacked out vehicles parked in front of the Highland Park mansion — the Rolls Royce Ghost that Grizzy had purchased shortly after receiving the $23 million from Johnna Broward, the Jeep Grand Cherokee Trailhawk that Grizzy had given to Marcus, and a Rolls Royce Cullinan that Nya had borrowed from Bulletface's underground garage.

Wearing smiles that spanned the entire widths of their gorgeous brown faces, Lacey and Nya climbed in the Cullinan, Nya in the passenger's seat with her mini-Draco on the floorboard in front of her five-inch, open-toe Louboutin heels and 40-caliber Glock 23 with a fifty-round drum magazine on her lap, Lacey behind the wheel with a 45-caliber Glock 30 on her lap.

Marcus and Grizzy slipped into the Ghost with their Dracos in hand, and the two Rolls Royces darted down the long driveway and out the slowly opening front gates.

"Bitch," Nya said tightly, "the next time you snitch on me, I'm fuckin' you up. Now try me if you want to."

Lacey snickered. "Okay, first off, I did not tell him about Quendell. Your mama told his mama. You know they exchanged numbers at the engagement party, and they talked after Willie White's memorial yesterday. My mama was on the phone too."

Nya rolled her eyes, feigning indignance. She was actually relieved, and seconds later, it showed. She brought up her drill playlist and pressed play on Lil Durk's *Mad Max*. She raised her phone and recorded a quick, twenty second video for her Instagram stories, showing off her glistening diamonds, vibing to music, with a mug on her face. She'd brought a small bottle of water along with her, and she kept taking sips from it as Lacey drove, her vigilant brown eyes scanning the streets around them.

After a few minutes, she lowered the music volume and addressed the obvious.

"So," she said, "that $5 million, what's your thoughts on it?"

"I think it's dangerous as fuck for your husband right now," Lacey said quickly. "He should've listened to Bam. I wouldn't dare come outside if somebody had that much money on my head. Shiiiit. Fuck that. I'd be in Utah somewhere. Ain't no way in hell I'd still be in Chicago, especially if I had the kinda money you and Grizzy got."

"Nahhh." Nya shook her head. "Ain't no runnin'. We out here. Fuck Johnna and her punk ass brother." She sipped some more water and then added, "Plus, you know Bang Boy paid a million dollars to get Grizzy's daddy killed in that federal prison. You saw how Grizzy cried at the funeral service yesterday. I'm pretty sure he'd rather die than to run. It's personal for him, so it's personal for me too."

It was Lacey's turn to shake her head. Her blond curls swayed as she did it. She wore a tight, black, Dolce and Gabbana dress with a slit up the right thigh and three-inch Louboutin heels.

"Look at how many celebrities left the city when they made it," she said. "Lil Durk left. King Van left. Herbo left. Chief Keef left. Leaving ain't necessarily running. You'll always be from Chicago. But why in the fuck would Grizzy stay here when y'all know somebody got $5 *million* on his head? Leaving because of that would be *smart*. And shit, what more do you have to prove anyway? You done stepped on everybody. What we got, two opps left?" Lacey chuckled once. "Bryce scared to death, and ain't nobody seen Jabar since we found out where he lived."

"Nah, we got a rich opp now," Nya said, watching a darkly tinted Hyundai Tucson that was passing them on the passenger's side. She picked up her Glock and discreetly aimed it at her door. Just in case.

"Yeah, but that man is way out in California," Lacey said. "I saw it on *The Shade Room*. Johnna bought Jim Carrey's Brentwood mansion and gave it to Bang Boy. They say she gave him $100 million when he got out of prison."

"Exactly. That's the most dangerous part about it. He can afford to pay $5 million to get somebody killed here in Chicago while he's kicked back on the west coast. I guarantee that after the FaceTime call he made to those gang leaders, at least eighty or ninety niggas loaded up and went on the hunt for Grizzy. Some of 'em gon' be at The Visionary Lounge when we get there."

"Yeah, well, all of Grizzy's boys gon' be there too. Marcus called them when y'all went to the bedroom. They're already in VIP. Branca, Spazz, Smoke, and a bunch of other niggas. And they got some more GDs posted up outside the club with about fifty guns. Brielle's at work, and Niecy couldn't find a babysitter, but Quita and Noesha said they're on the way to the club now. We'll be good."

Nya nodded her head. She went to thinking about the show. It had her more than a little anxious. She'd never performed in front of a crowd, and the fact that she would be performing at The Visionary Lounge, which was right in the middle of the west side neighborhood she'd grown up in, had her worried. It wasn't that she was afraid of rapping onstage while looking at many of the people she'd known since she was a kid. No, the anxiety was from the murders she and Grizzy had committed in the Austin neighborhood and the revenge seeking gang members who were almost certainly waiting for them to show their faces. The Visionary Lounge stood at the intersection of Chicago Avenue and Laramie, smack dab in the middle of Cold Gang territory. Nya had murdered Sleet, the original leader of Cold Gang, and she and Grizzy had paid Smoke $100,000 to down Frenchy, the man who'd taken the reigns after Sleet was killed. Cold Gang was on their third chief in less than two months, and it was all because of Nya and Grizzy.

"Can't lie," Lacey said, snatching Nya from her reverie, "when Marcus started texting people, at first, I thought he might be tryna collect on that $5 million. I got suspicious for a minute there. Then, Smoke called, and I relaxed."

Nya furrowed her brow, spun around in her seat to look back at the Rolls Royce Ghost trailing behind them, and eyed the other vehicles on the road with them. When she turned back to look at Lacey, she squinted her eyelids, holding the handle of her Glock tight in her fist, her forefinger resting on the trigger.

"I'll fuck your boyfriend up," Nya muttered threateningly. "He bet not dream of doin' some shit like that."

Lacey glanced over at Nya with a slight smile on her face, but the hint of a smile vanished the moment she caught sight of Nya's gelid expression. Her eyes returned to the road, and she said, "Calm the fuck down."

Nya looked away. Settling her gaze on a purple Dodge Magnum full of young niggas, she wondered how many people knew about the $5 million Bang Boy was offering for Grizzy's murder. Bryce knew, and he was bound to tell everyone else, if only to get some help. He knew he was in danger. He'd FaceTimed Nya to squash the beef, and she'd stared at him — coldly and silently — before ending the call.

The boys in the Magnum started looking at the two black Rolls Royces, so Nya stopped thinking about Bryce and started looking at them. The Magnum had huge rims and tinted windows, but the windows were all halfway down, so Nya lowered hers halfway and reached down to pick up her mini-Draco.

They were on Roosevelt Road, cruising along at a steady forty miles per hour. There was a police car several car lengths ahead of them. The driver of the Dodge Magnum seemed to be focused on it. He had stringy dreads hanging down around his head. The other passengers had stopped looking at the Cullinan and were focused solely on the Ghost.

"You ever seen this Magnum before?" Nya asked.

Lacey was slowing for a red traffic light at the intersection of Roosevelt and Kedzie when she glanced over at the Magnum. The Rolls Royces were in the left lane, preparing to make a left turn, and the Magnum fell in line behind them to make the same turn.

"Probably just some Travelers from over this way," Lacey guessed, meaning Traveling Vice Lords. They had just entered the west side's North Lawndale neighborhood, Dark Side TVL territory.

Bam was the *chief* of the Dark Side TVLs.

"I swear to God, Lacey," Nya said, holding her mini-Draco in a death grip and rising up to peer over the back of her seat, "if these niggas get on some bullshit with my husband, I'm crashin' out."

"Girl, stop being so paranoid. They're lookin' at two black Rolls Royces. They probably think it's Lil Durk or some'n. If you didn't wanna draw no attention, then maybe we should've drove here in the Trackhawk."

Shaking her head skeptically, Nya narrowed her eyelids and stared at her sideview mirror.

"They can't see Grizzy anyway." Lacey went on. "He's in the backseat with the curtains drawn. They would have to know he's back there to…"

Nya gasped as the Magnum suddenly veered into view in her sideview mirror. It bumped up onto the curb and sped up alongside the Rolls Royce Ghost. Two arms came out the driver's side windows holding black pistols with extended clips, and before Nya could maneuver in her seat and reach out her window with the Draco, fully automatic gunfire was already spewing from the barrels of their guns. They emptied their thirty-round clips in two seconds. By then, Nya was hanging out her window, firing into the Magnum's front windshield. She saw the driver jerk back in his seat as a barrage of 7.62-millimeter rounds slammed through him. Marcus swerved around the Cullinan and shot past them, and Lacey sped off after him.

"No! Stop!" Nya screamed, but Lacey kept driving. Speeding. Rocketing southbound down Kedzie Avenue. Nya continued shooting until she lost sight of the Magnum, and then, she slithered back down into her seat and glowered at Lacey before turning her attention to the Rolls Royce sedan they were chasing behind.

Then, she lifted her Draco and aimed the smoking barrel at the side of Lacey's head.

Lacey's eyes got big. "Nya, what the fuck is wrong with..."

"Turn around!" Nya ordered "Go back! Either that or stop here and get out and I'll go back myself."

"Bitch, the fuckin' police will be there waitin' on us if we go back. We need to make sure Grizzy's okay."

Just then, Nya's phone lit up with a call from Marcus. She answered the call, and Marcus's frantic voice came through the Cullinan's speaker system.

"They hit Grizzy!" Marcus shouted. "Shit, man, he ain't movin'. They hit him everywhere. Where the closest hospital?"

Nya fell forward, her forehead smacking the dashboard. She hardly felt it. Her eyes filled with tears, and she cried for a long while.

Chapter 5

Panteon Tech headquarters in Lower Manhattan officially reopened the morning of Wednesday, July 5th, 2023, exactly six weeks and one day after a disgruntled former employee stormed into the five-story office building and snuffed out four innocent lives with a military-style assault rifle.

Johnna Broward had spent over $150 million compensating the families of the victims. She'd boasted Panteon's three-man team of armed security guards to a thirty-man crew, most of them former members of the NYPD. There were guard shacks and barricades at both vehicular entrances. There were mandatory ID checks and bullet-resistant and automated locking mechanisms on every door, the whole nine yards. Johnna and her wealthy board of executives weren't taking any chances. The Panteon shooting had made international news. Although support from the global community had sent sales of Panteon home security systems through the roof, Johnna was grimly determined to prevent the next workplace shooting from ever taking place.

There were several traumatized Panteon employees who'd opted out of returning to the office. They were easily replaced. The average salary at Panteon Technologies was $118,500 a year, and there were literally hundreds of job applications submitted every month.

When Johnna finally made it to her top-floor office with Tiffany "Tip" Stingley, her newest personal assistant, following closely behind her, she paused in the doorway and stared at the spot on her floor where Michael Caldwell, the unhinged workplace shooter, had mashed her face into the carpet and threatened to shoot her in the back of the head if she didn't answer his question.

He'd wanted to know where she was hiding the $23 million in drug money she'd stolen from his old friend, Butch Gibbs, millions of dollars in cash that Butch himself had stolen from an incarcerated heroin kingpin named Willie White. Unbeknownst to Michael Caldwell, he'd actually been *standing* in the money. Johnna had spent close to a million dollars paying off her collage loans, moving her family out of the ghetto, and getting herself settled in New York City, and she'd used the remaining $22 million to create Panteon Technologies in early 2018. By the time Caldwell burst into her office six weeks ago, Johnna's net worth had already risen to nearly three billion dollars.

And now, just forty-three days later, her net worth had skyrocketed to $14.3 billion.

"It's hard coming back, ain't it?" Tip asked.

Johnna nodded her head solemnly, took a deep breath, and stepped into her office, taking a moment to study the new white carpeting. Her former security guard and ex-boyfriend, Jayvon Sullivan, had splattered blood, brain matter, and skull fragments all across the old carpet when he shot Michael Caldwell in the head from the open doorway. The macabre memory of it made Johnna cringe, but somehow, she managed to reach the swivel chair behind her new glass desk and plop her surgically enhanced butt down onto the richly upholstered leather.

Tip sat in one of the two armchairs in front of the desk and brought up Johnna's itinerary on her phone, and while she chattered her way through a list of scheduled boardroom meetings and Zoom meetings and conference calls, Johnna leaned back in her chair and looked at the attractive young woman.

Light brown in complexion and naturally curvy below the waist, with a short bob of neatly arranged, dark hair, and a gorgeous smile, Tiffany Stingley was a Midwest girl who, despite being in the corporate world, still carried herself like a project chick from the trenches. She'd been employed as one of Panteon's lower-level accountants until she witnessed Johnna beat the living daylights out of Michael Caldwell's wife, Diana, on the morning of the shooting. Diana had pressed charges against Johnna and filed a lawsuit against Panteon. She'd attempted to use Tip as an eyewitness, so Johnna had promoted Tip to her personal assistant, boosting her annual salary from $127,000 to $315,000, and Tip had come down with a sudden case of amnesia when the district attorney called her in for questioning. She'd taken a strong dose of pain medicine that morning, she claimed. She'd heard Diana Martin-Caldwell mutter threats, saying she was going to punch Johnna in the face for firing her husband, but she couldn't remember much else. It was all a fog, and the trauma of the shooting that went down hours later had thickened the fog.

Diana had thrown a fit, and Johnna had thrown a yacht party.

"Thanks for helping me out of that jam," Johnna said when Tip looked up from her phone. "I truly do appreciate it. Diana tried to ruin me, but you came through."

Tip lowered her phone and smiled. "Girl, fuck Diana. I don't know where she's from, but where I come from, we don't cooperate with the police. She should've kept that shit in the streets. She tried to tell me she was doing it for the money, cause you're a billionaire, but that ain't got nothin' to do with it. I don't care if you was a trillionaire. I ain't snitchin' on nobody. A bitch like her wouldn't make it one day in Gary."

Johnna laughed. "Gary, Indiana?" And when Tip nodded her head yes, Johnna said, "I know some girls from out there. Chauntine from Fifth Avenue and her auntie, Taske. My brother used to date Chauntine. Her brother was one of those Fifth Avenue Boyz, and her uncles were all GDs from Edna. "Joka Mo" or something like that. What made you move to New York?"

"Money," Tip answered frankly. "My cousin was from here. She went missing in Mexico some years ago, but she used to be best friends with Alexus Costilla. I figured since she was from here and ended up friends with the richest person on Earth, I figured I might as well come out here and see what I could come up on."

Another laugh from Johnna. "Well," she said, "you didn't do too bad. I might not have $223 billion like Alexus, but I'm doing okay."

They were sharing a laugh when Johnna's phone rang. It was a call from her big brother. She looked up at Tip, thinking up an excuse to get rid of her for a couple of minutes, but Tip seemed to read her mind.

"I'll go and find Kiara," Tip said, meaning Kiara Barrington, Panteon Tech's chief financial officer and Johnna's first meeting of the day.

Johnna nodded her head and waited for Tip to exit her office before accepting the video call. She positioned the iPhone against a coffee mug on her desk and stared fixedly at her incredibly handsome older brother. Johnny "Bang Boy" Broward was walking through his Brentwood mansion, the flawless, white diamonds on his teeth sparkling brilliantly in the light. Celebrity jeweler Johnny Dang had charged him $100,000 for the icy grill — $5,000 per tooth. His skin complexion was pecan brown like Johnna's. His dreads were colored red at the tips, and they hung down around his head like strings of yarn. He had fat, round, white diamonds in his earlobes and five diamond necklaces around his tattooed neck.

"I know you done heard the news," he said, beaming.

Johnna shook her head no "What news?"

He switched to his rear camera, and suddenly, Johnna was looking at two curvaceous, young, Instagram models — one a sexy, tatted-up Latina in a red, lace thong and no bra, the other a long haired, chocolate girl wearing nothing at all. They were lying in Johnny's bed, the Hispanic one holding a smartphone in one hand.

"Read that out loud for my sister," Bang Boy said.

"Okay," said the stunningly attractive Latina. "This is from an ABC7 news article that was posted a few hours ago. Chicago rapper Young Nya's husband was reportedly gunned down on the city's west side late last night. Investigators say thirty-seven-year-old Lejon Kamari White was shot at least forty-one times while riding in the backseat of a Rolls Royce sedan in the North Lawndale neighborhood. He'd been en route to what would have been Young Nya's first ever live performance, which was set to take place at The Visionary Lounge, when a dark-colored Dodge Magnum pulled up next to his car and opened fire. Someone in his entourage reportedly shot and killed the nineteen-year-old driver of the Magnum, and the other alleged gunman fled the area on foot before police arrived on scene..."

"There's more, but that's the gist of it. TMZ just posted a video showing Young Nya crying and hugging her friend, Lacey, outside the emergency room. She never did the show." Johnny switched back to the front facing camera as he turned around and left his bedroom, and for a few seconds, he and Johnna just smiled at each other. A great wave of relief swept through Johnna in that moment. She'd learned from a billionaire friend of hers that the FBI had started investigating her over the $23 million she'd sent to Lejon White to dead the issue between her and his father.

But all that was over now. Willie White and his son, Lejon, were dead. So was Butch. There was only one more person who posed a threat to Johnna's multi-billion-dollar empire, and her name was Diana Martin-Caldwell.

As if on cue, Johnny said, "So, what's up with this Diana chick?"

"She's a problem," Johnna said, sitting forward. "She was married to Michael Caldwell, and I'm almost positive he told her about the money from Butch. If she gives that information to the Feds, they'll have reason to raid all of my properties, my offices — everything. They'll subpoena emails. I went through and deleted all the emails from Butch, but they might be able to recover them."

"So, where can I find Diana?"

"She has an apartment in East Brooklyn, but she's been staying with her son in Queens. I can send you the address. My assistant has it. She's solid. We can trust her."

Johnny nodded once. "You know," he said, lighting a cigarette, "that nigga, Grizzy, got snaked by somebody in his own circle. I got two niggas tryna collect that $5 million I dropped on his head. This fat nigga named U.T. claim he had one do it, but Mandré had another nigga hit him up on FaceTime when they shot up that Rolls Royce. He's supposed to be splittin' the money with one of Grizzy's people."

"So, who are you gonna pay?"

"Shit, the nigga who did it. He showed proof. Plus, he had the inside scoop. He knew Grizzy was in the backseat with the curtain closed. I gotta pay him. U.T. ain't do shit as far as I could tell. I think what happened was he tried to get one of his lil homies to do it, so he could keep most of the money and pay them just a few hundred bands, but they went behind his back and reached out to somebody in Grizzy's circle. Found out how much was really being offered. They probably agreed to split the money."

"Well," Johnna said with a note of finality, "go ahead and pay them so we can focus all energy on Diana."

Johnna had booted up her desktop computer and was reading the ABC7 News article for herself. There was a video that went with it. ABC7 News anchor woman Val

Warner was sitting behind a news desk, breaking the news of the deadly shooting, while footage of police shining their flashlights on Lejon White's bullet-riddled Rolls Royce played on the opposite side of the screen.

"I'll be there in New York later on this evening," Johnny said.

"Okay. And leave those girls where you found them. I don't need them rubbing their naked asses all over the seats on my jet. I paid almost $52 million for that G650. Show it some respect."

Johnny was chuckling and shaking his head as he ended the video call, and ten seconds later, Kiara and Tip walked into Johnna's spacious office, both of them smiling like the rest of Panteon's first shift employees, glad to be back in the building.

Johnna was glad too. She loved work. Loved it more than life itself. Panteon was her brain child. Through the grace of God, she'd been able to turn dozens of suitcases full of wrinkled, rubber-banded stacks of drug money into one of the top five tech companies in the industry. Now that her big brother had won his appeal, freeing him from the Federal Bureau of Prisons, she had the backing of a real gangster she could entrust with doing the dirty work of eradicating the last remaining threats to her lucrative empire. Then, she and her family would be able to relax and enjoy the fruits of her labor for generations to come.

Bang Boy had already succeeded in taking out Grizzy and Willie White. Once Diana was out of the picture, Johnna would be unstoppable.

Which could only mean one thing: Diana Martin-Caldwell's days were numbered.

Chapter 6

Diana Martin-Caldwell had been staying with her oldest son, Rock, and his family in their four-bedroom townhouse at 212-55 Jamaica Avenue in Queens, New York, but she didn't want to risk the address leaking to the news media, so she had NYPD detectives, Richard McKenzie and Erica Sinclair, meet her at the corner of 214th Place and 94th Road, and she got in the back of their blacked-out Expedition.

"We could've just picked you up from home," McKenzie said, turning in the front passenger seat to look back at Diana.

She regarded him skeptically. He was an older white man, slender and silver-haired, with piercing blue eyes and an overly friendly demeanor that probably worked for him in his line of work. But it didn't work on Diana. A lifelong resident of East Brooklyn's Canarsie and Brownsville neighborhoods, she knew how the NYPD operated. Even the nice ones like McKenzie. Deep down, he was just as cold as the others, his heart frozen solid like the two-month-old lamb chops in Diana's deep freezer.

"What's going on with your lawsuit?" Sinclair asked. She was a Black woman, early thirties, as frigid on the outside as her partner was on the inside. "I read somewhere that you were seeking $250 million from Panteon."

The thought of that much money brightened Diana's spirits. The meaty corners of her mouth inched upward, and she said, "They haven't made offers yet, but they settled pretty quickly with the families of the shooting victims. Tabby Green's family got $100 million. My lawyer thinks an offer may be weeks or even days away."

"You're looking a heck of a lot better than you did when we first saw you," Sinclair commented as she sliced through traffic.

And boy was she right. When they'd come knocking at Diana's apartment door six weeks ago, she'd been reclined in her deceased husband's favorite armchair with her head tilted back, her eyes squeezed shut, and the short barrel of a chrome-plated revolver wedged between her chattering teeth. Had the detectives arrived just five seconds later, Diana's brains would have been dripping down her living room wall, and she would have been in Heaven with her dearly departed husband. She'd answered the door dressed in the same outfit she had worn to work the day before, the scratches on her chubby face from her fight with Johnna Broward wet and shiny with antibacterial ointment, the collar of her blouse torn and bloodied.

Now she looked like an entirely different woman. She'd lost at least twenty pounds. Rock's wife, Cara, was a makeup artist for their funeral business, and she'd done an exceptional job of revamping her mother-in-law's look. Diana's real hair was braided down underneath an expensive, lace front wig of shimmery, shoulder-length blonde curls, and she wore a cute, pink, Palm Angels jogger over Nike Air Max sneakers of the same color. Rock and Cara had practically bought her a whole new wardrobe, and though they claimed to have done it to help her through the trauma of losing Michael, she knew their true motive.

Like everyone else in Diana's rapidly growing circle of family and friends, they wanted in on the money she was about to get from the lawsuit she'd filed against Johnna Broward and Panteon Technologies.

"Thank you," Diana said to the leggy young female detective. "What was it you two wanted to speak with me about? Not to be rude or anything, but I have an appointment at noon."

McKenzie turned in his seat again. "You might be in danger," he said.

"Danger? What kinda danger?"

McKenzie's nostrils flared as he drew in a deep, nasal breath. He blew it out his mouth and took off his eyeglasses. "Johnna Broward may be a lot more dangerous than initially believed. In fact, I'm certain she is. You'd think Johnna was the boss of some sort of Russian crime family, the way her rivals keep getting knocked off. I wouldn't want to be on her shit list."

Diana knitted her brow. "Okay, I'm thoroughly lost now. Who has she gotten killed? Somebody from Panteon?" And before he could give an answer, she said, "I believe she paid Tiffany Stingley to say I threatened her before the fight, but I don't see Johnna getting anybody *killed*. She's a bitch, but she ain't *that* big of a bitch."

Detective Sinclair slowed to a stop outside a Starbucks. She asked Diana what kind of coffee she drank, and apparently, she was already aware of McKenzie's preferred flavor because she got out without asking him and went inside.

"Quick question," McKenzie said. "You ever hear anything about Johnna stealing drug money from a Chicago gang leader named Willie White?"

Diana's eyebrows shot up to her forehead. Her lips parted with an audible pop as something Michael had told her during a romantic dinner just a couple of months ago flashed across her mind's eye.

He'd told her that he was a former member of a Chicago street gang called the Almighty Black P. Stones and that the particular faction he'd been a part of — the "White Moes" that had operated within and around the Altgeld Gardens Housing Complex on Chicago's far south side — was led by a man named Willie White, a "general" for the gang who'd been busted with ninety-one kilos of heroin and well over $800,000 in cash when a joint task force of Chicago policemen and FBI, DEA, and ATF agents began raiding homes and businesses associated with the gang in late 2004 and early 2005. At the time, another White Moe called Butch had been in possession of approximately $30 million in illicit drug money the gang had accumulated from heroin and crack-cocaine sales on Chicago's far south side.

In exchange for lighter sentencing, Michael and Butch had cooperated with federal investigators, detailing everything from the gang's strict hierarchy to the gang's elaborate drug dealing empire and the numerous homicides certain members had committed over the years, but the thing they had *not* mentioned was the $30 million.

Butch was eventually released from federal prison after serving twelve years in protective custody. Michael had done seventeen years in similar conditions, and when he got out, he'd learned from Butch that Johnna Broward, the younger sister of one of the White Moes' most dangerous men — a ruthless killer named Johnny "Bang Boy" Broward — had drugged Butch and escaped with the majority of the money in September of 2017. Hoping to recover at least some of the stolen drug money, Michael had secured a job as a night shift janitor at Panteon Tech's Lower Manhattan headquarters where he'd worked for several months before he was caught on camera snooping around inside Johnna's office. He'd been fired for the transgression, which had led to Diana and Johnna's hallway brawl three days later and Michael's deadly shooting spree a few hours after that.

The vivid memory of Michael's jaw-dropping revelation came and went in a couple of seconds, but the inquisitive look on McKenzie's face showed that he'd picked up on it. His eyes were stringent slits. He'd put his glasses back on, and he was staring at Diana as if he suspected her of being the culprit behind a rash of unsolved bank robberies.

"So, I take it you have heard about the stolen drug money?" he said slowly, watchfully.

Diana hesitated. Then, "Look, I may know a bit more than I told you, but I wanna keep that to myself for now. For leverage. Maybe it'll pressure Johnna and her lawyers into offering me a decent settlement."

"Hm." McKenzie nodded his narrow head. "I think that might've been what Butch Gibbs had in mind before he went missing. His charred remains were found two days ago in the basement of some abandoned house in Gary, Indiana."

Diana's mouth popped open again.

"Oh, you know him?" McKenzie asked.

It took Diana a moment to compose herself. "I, uh... yeah. I've heard of him. He and Michael grew up together."

"Yeah, well, according to the missing person's report Butch's wife filed with the Chicago Police Department, he told her that Johnna Broward had stolen $23 million in drug money from him back in 2017 and that she'd only paid him back a million dollars. To make amends, Johnna sent Butch and his family on a Brazilian vacation, and she was supposed to be wiring him at least $10 million when they returned home to Chicago three weeks later, but he went missing shortly after the private jet landed at O'Hare, and no one saw him again until he was found burned and shot in the head two days ago."

"Jesus Christ," Diana murmured.

"And Willie White," the silver-hair detective went on, "the guy who the drug money initially belonged to, was murdered in federal prison about a week ago, just days after he got into a fight with Johnna's older brother, who was released from that fed joint three days after Willie's murder. He was believed to be the main shooter in Willie White's organization, but somehow, he managed to get his life sentence overturned on appeal. There's a bank statement floating around that proves Johnna sent exactly $23 million to Lejon White, Willie White's son, the very same night that

Willie and her brother, Bang Boy, got in that fight. And last night, Lejon White was shot forty-one times while riding in the back of a Rolls Royce, Word on the street is that Bang Boy put $5 million on his head."

Diana sat, staring at McKenzie for a long moment. He stared back at her, his subtle smirk a triumphant one. He'd succeeded in scaring the living daylights out of her, and he knew it.

But maybe he was right. After all, Johana was related to Bang Boy. Everyone at Panteon had spoken about it when Johnna wasn't around. Bang Boy had been charged with seven gang murders. Now that he was free from prison, it was very plausible that he had gone back to his old ways, and there was no way of telling what he would do if and when he ever learned of Diana's spat with his sister.

"I'd advise you to come clean with us," McKenzie said. "It won't affect your lawsuit. If anything, it'll *help* your case. Prove that Johnna's a criminal who deserves to be put away. If we can prove that she actually did use Willie White's drug money to start Panteon, it would ruin her. She'd be forced into selling her majority stake in the company, and she'd likely do a considerable amount of prison time for money laundering, misleading investors, and lying to the IRS. She could even be held liable for the Panteon shooting."

Shaking her head, Diana scooched across the seat, pushed open her door, and stepped out onto the curb. "I'll call you," she said as Detective Sinclair walked behind her. "I need to talk with my lawyer about this first."

She accepted the coffee from Sinclair, thanked her, and then went inside the Starbucks. She sat down and took out her phone. She canceled her noon massage appointment, ordered an Uber, and phoned Tip Stingley, the former Panteon coworker of hers who'd been one of her closest friends until her fight with Johnna. She didn't get an answer (That was no huge surprise there; Tip hadn't answered her calls in weeks), so she went on Instagram, found Johnny

"Bang Boy" Broward's page, and spent several minutes watching videos of him lounging around his gorgeous hilltop mansion, hanging out with his gang on a private jet, and showing off newly purchased jewelry and exotic vehicles.

There was one video in particular that really got to Diana. It showed Bang Boy and his four friends at a gun range, each one of them firing an assault rifle with a drum magazine at their paper targets. They handled the weapons like elite military men, only they were dressed like wealthy gang members, hard-eyed men with ink on their faces and arms and diamonds on their necks and wrists.

It was at that point when Diana had a premonition of Bang Boy and his gang firing off their assault rifles in her direction, those red-hot bullets spiraling through her flesh, blasting open her organs, deflating her lungs — ending her very existence.

With trembling fingers, she exited the Instagram app and dialed Detective McKenzie's phone number, and when he answered, she muttered three quick words.

"Okay," she said. "I'm in."

Chapter 7

Bryce Webb used one finger to discreetly push down a venetian blind and peek out to the gangway alongside his girlfriend, Raven's house. He looked toward the back and saw no one. Looked toward the front and caught a glimpse of a neighbor's seven-year-old boy running past the wrought-iron fence with a Super Soaker water gun in hand.

Next, Bryce went to the Panteon Home Security app on his phone and studied the live video feeds from all four exterior cameras — the two on the front and back porches, the one positioned just under the roof behind the house, and the one positioned right outside his son's upstairs bedroom window at the front of the house. There were six little kids playing with water guns and water balloons on the sidewalk out front, no activity in the fenced in backyard, two boys dealing drugs outside the garage in the gravel alleyway out back, and a teenage couple walking hand-in-hand down the length of the alley. Nothing to be concerned over.

Bryce pocketed his phone, but he kept his Glock 19 in hand, just as he'd done every day for the past few weeks. He hated to admit it, but he was in fear for his life, and it was all because of a 4'10" female. It was not that height had anything to do with the threat. Bullets fired from a small woman had the same effect as bullets fired from a large man, and Nya Mixon was the most trigger-happy little woman the west side of Chicago had ever birthed.

Bryce returned to the living room sofa, put his gun down on the coffee table, and took a huge bite out of his Italian beef sandwich. He ate a couple of French fries and smiled when he looked up at the seventy-inch smart TV and saw ABC7 News anchor Val Warner talking about Nya's husband being shot to death late last night.

The low sound of Latto's *Another Nasty Song* made him flick his eyes over to the hallway. It was one of the songs Raven liked dancing to at the strip club. She'd turned her spare bedroom into a pole dancing room, complete with a golden pole bolted to the hardwood floor in the center of the room, a smart speaker in one corner, and a tripod she set her smartphone on to stream video to her Only Fans subscribers.

Bryce took another bite from his sandwich, chased it down with a swallow of grape Crush soda, and picked up his gun. He checked the Panteon app again and saw that his younger cousin, Jabar's tan-colored Chevy Impala had just pulled up and parked behind Raven's cherry-red Mercedes Benz G-Wagon. Jabar got out of the car, carrying a plain gray backpack on one shoulder. Bryce's eyes lit up at the sight of it because he knew what the backpack contained. It was the money from the four drug spots he'd taken over as the newest leader of Cold Gang. He was making between $15,000 and $20,000 per day, and although a lot of it went right back to Bam — the man who, for years, had supplied Cold Gang with kilos of cocaine, heroin, fentanyl, and meth — Bryce always had a few grand left over to blow. He spent a lot of it on guns and ammunition and on lawyers and commissary for his incarcerated gang members, but he'd also purchased a foreclosed house that was currently under renovation, and he'd put a fresh set of twenty-six-inch Forgiato rims on his 7-Series BMW.

He got up and went to the door to let Jabar in, and after he secured the deadbolt, the two of them went to the sofa and recounted the cash to make sure it was the same amount the worker had told him it was.

It was all there. $12,850 in ones, fives, tens, twenties, fifties, and hundreds, and about seventy dollars in loose change. It was a good thing Raven was a stripper. She could deposit Bryce's dirty dollars into her bank account and withdraw it as new hundreds and twenties. Which was what she did for him all the time.

"Where Raven at?" Jabar asked.

"She back there dancing for Only Fans. Ol' money hungry ass bitch."

Jahar chuckled aloud. He was a slender young man who hadn't been an official member of Cold Gang until a week ago, though he'd been in the mix for years. Bryce had made him a Three Star Branch Elite and put him in charge of delivering the drugs to his trap spots at the beginning of every shift and bringing the money back to Bryce at the end of the shift.

Bryce handed Jabar $300 in twenties and left the rest of the cash piled on the table.

"What happened with you and Raven?" Jabar asked, pocketing the cash and bringing out a sack of exotic weed. "I saw it on IG. She posted a pic with a caption that said, 'Fuck Nigga Free.' That mean she single. Y'all must've got into it again."

Bryce nodded his head and told Jabar about his beef with Raven. She was contracted to work exclusively at Bankroll Reese's strip clubs, and since Redbone's Gentlemen's Club had shut down after Frenchy, Wobble, and Curry were gunned down in the parking lot a week and a half ago, Raven was temporarily out of work. The monthly payments on her G-Wagon exceeded two thousand dollars. Her mortgage was another two grand. She paid all of her mother's rent and utilities and, on top of that, a portion of her younger sister's bills, and she had her mother and two siblings on her phone plan. She'd asked Bryce to help her out with all the bills, and he'd said no because he knew that she would've had the money had she not blown $11,000 on a Louis Vuitton dress and another $19,000 on a diamond Chanel necklace two weeks ago. She had $77,000 of Bryce's money in her bank account and was pissed that he wouldn't let her get the odd $7,000.

"Man, give her that money," Jabar said, rolling a blunt. "II it wasn't for her, you wouldn't be able to wash all that dirty money in the first place."

"Fuck that bitch. She better ask Bankroll Reese for some money. Shit, he told her she could fly down to Miami or Vegas and work at one of the strip clubs he got down there. I'll pay for the plane ticket. That's about it. Fuck I look like, a trick or some'n?"

"It ain't trickin' if you got it, Lord," Jabar reasoned.

Bryce waved him off and finished off the rest of his sandwich. He knew he could afford to give_Raven the $7,000, but he'd put $50,000 on Nya's head, and if one of his shooters happened to catch Nya outside and put a few bullets in her head today, he would have to pay up.

And make no mistake about it, getting rid of Nya Mixon was more important than anything else he had going on at the moment.

There were literally hundreds upon hundreds of people trolling Bryce on social media over the losses his faction of Conservative Vice Lords had taken at the hands of Nya and her husband — and most of the gossipmongers didn't even mention the husband. They were saying that Nya, and only Nya, was responsible for the deaths of Sleet, Sleet's nephew, Devin, Frenchy, Sticks, Nardo, Mikey, Derrick, and Dre. Not to mention the seven Wicked Town TVLs she was rumored to have murdered (Wobble, Crunchy, Curry, and the four teenage boys who were caught lacking at a red light after the strip club shooting) and the two Four Corner Hustlers who were shot and killed near her father's west side home. That was *seventeen murders.*

Bottom line: Nya Mixon had to go, and Bryce was determined to make it happen.

Jabar put fire to the end of his blunt. Bryce downed the last of his grape soda and belched just as Raven came sauntering into the living room wearing only a towering pair of see-through heals, a pink, lace thong, and a matching bra. The pierced nipples of her D-cup breasts were visible through the lace. She had a reddish-brown complexion with freckles on her round, sexy face and a big, bubble butt that had made her a few hundred thousand dollars over the years. Her skin was shiny with body oil. She wore false eyelashes and a blonde wig with red highlights that ran down her back like a colorful waterfall. She held her iPhone in one hand, and she didn't look up from it as she marched through the living room with her fat, round butt cheeks jiggling unrestrainedly.

"What's up, Rave?" Jabar said croakily; he had just inhaled, and his lungs were filled with the potent smoke.

Raven responded with a flutter of her professionally manicured fingernails and continued on into the kitchen without looking back at them. Jabar laughed at her cantankerous attitude and shook his head. He said they were crazy, and then, he passed the blunt and asked him where they were hiding Bryce Jr.

"She sent him off to summer camp, so she could slut around for six weeks,'" Bryce said, loud enough for Raven to hear him.

She sucked her teeth and flipped him a middle finger as she pulled open her stainless-steel smart fridge. She stood there a moment, typing on her phone. Which reminded Bryce to take another look at the Panteon app.

He picked up his phone and went to the app, only to find that he'd been logged out. He typed in the password and was told he'd entered the wrong one.

"The fuck?" Bryce muttered. He looked over at Raven. She had just shut the fridge and was cracking open a tall bottle of Fiji water. "You changed the Panteon password?"

"Sure in the hell did. I pay nineteen dollars and ninety-nine cents every goddamn month for that subscription," Raven said. "If you can't put in on it, you can't fuckin' use it. Ol'_scary ass bitch."

Bryce clenched his teeth and glowered at her. He was a 5'6", high yellow nigga with a serious case of Napoleon complex. He hit the blunt and turned back to Jabar, shaking his head in frustration.

"On Sleet," he said, "this bitch gon' fuck around and make me slap them fake ass lashes off her face."

In an attempt to change the subject, Jabar said, "I see somebody caught up with that nigga, Grizzy, and got that $5 million. Wish they would've hit Nya up too. They say she hung out the window and whacked Lil Pistol. Shot him all in his face with a Draco. Shorty ain't for none. I ain't lie. I wanna kill that lil bitch, but you gotta respect her gangsta. She applyin' pressure."

Bryce heard Jabar's words, but they hardly registered. He was staring at the money on Raven's coffee table. With all the bills of lower denominations, the remaining $12,500 looked more like $80,000. But that wasn't what Bryce's eyes had locked on to. It was the stacks of coins that had his undivided attention.

He picked up two piles of quarters and launched them at Raven. Many of them struck her in the side of the head.

"You want some money, bitch?! You want nineteen dollars? Hm?"

Bryce was reaching for another stack of coins when Raven's cold bottle of water slapped him hard across the face. The impact rocked his head, infuriating him, and he started to run at her. But Raven was fast. She dashed across the kitchen and snatched a nine-inch butcher knife from a drawer. "Run up if you want to." She dared him.

Bryce launched another fistful of coins, and Raven ducked them like a character from *The Matrix* as Jabar wrapped his arms around Bryce and pulled him toward the front door.

"Chill out, Lord," Jabar said, his mouth close to Bryce's ear. "Let's step outside for a minute, get sum air. Y'all trippin', fam."

"Nah, I ain't trippin'," Raven replied snappishly. "Both of y'all can get the fuck out my house. Got me fucked up." She had tears in her eyes, but she looked angry. She held the butcher knife in an iron grip, and as Jabar dragged Bryce closer to the door, she moved forward and scooped up Bryce's Glock from the table.

She didn't point it at them, but the sight of it in her hand calmed Bryce enough to stop him from struggling against Jabar's bear hug. He turned toward the door, furious, and two seconds later, he and Jabar walked out onto the front porch.

It was a hot summer day, ninety-four degrees. The heat hit Bryce like a wall of fire, sucking all the air out of him. The cocaine he'd snorted less than an hour ago made him even hotter. He'd pledged to give up his cocaine habit months ago, and for a while, he'd succeeded. But the overwhelming stress of dealing with grieving families of the men Nya and her people had sent to the grave had him on edge night and day, and powder cocaine was the only thing that could keep him alert and fearless in the face of constant danger.

Gritting his teeth, Bryce punched the black, metal mailbox next to Raven's front door and growled in the back of his throat.

"Come on," Jabar said. "Let's go for a ride real quick."

"I ain't got my pipe on me."

Jabar lifted the front of his Balmain tee shirt and showed the butt of his 9-millimeter Sig Sauer pistol. "We good, cuzzo. Let's slide for a minute. Give her some time to chill out."

Still glowering, Bryce dropped his head and started down the porch steps ahead of his cousin. They were on

Washington and Kostner, in Unknown Vice Lord territory, but they knew they were good. Bryce was a gang chief now. A shot-caller. He had tremendous pull, especially within the Almighty Vice Lord Nation. The clique of boys standing near the corner knew all about Bryce Webb, and he knew they wouldn't hesitate to pull their pistols if someone attempted to run down on him.

He threw open the wrought iron gate and stepped out onto the wet sidewalk, digging his BMW key out of his pocket, looking around. There was a tall, long-legged, dark-skinned girl in a light blue summer dress walking past the sidewalk across the street. Under normal circumstances, Bryce would have given her a shout, but he was much too heated to acknowledge beauty. He pressed the button to unlock his BMW 745 and walked around the back of his car to get to the driver door just as a blacked-out Dodge Challenger SRT Demon came down the street in his direction.

He had one hand on his door latch and was scowling at Raven's teasing smile as she stood looking out at him from her living room window when he heard the powerful 840-horsepower engine, and he turned to look just as the Demon came screeching to a stop right next to him.

The two women inside the muscle car wore pink ski masks over their faces, but Bryce had a pretty good idea who they were. The smaller one in the passenger seat — the one who had a mini-Draco with a drum magazine aimed at his face — was Nya Mixon, and the tall bitch in the driver's seat was her friend, Lacey.

Bryce ducked low and turned to run as Nya and Lacey pushed open their doors. He heard the thunderous rattle of a fully automatic gun going off and stumbled trying to flee around the rear of his BMW. He watched Jabar fall flat on his back as Lacey ran up on him, firing a Glock that had been modified to fire like a machine gun. Bryce tripped and fell down hard on one knee, swiveling his head to look back at

Nya. She was fast on her feet, standing behind him now, aiming the mini-Draco at his back.

He exhaled sharply as a three-round burst of 7.62-millimeter rifle rounds carved holes in his upper back. He reached out for the curb and tried to crawl toward Jabar, even as he watched fire boom from the barrel of Lacey's Glock and Jabar's head jerk around as fifteen or twenty shots from the Glock's fifty-round drum made a mess of his face.

Somehow, Bryce found the strength to roll over on his back half a second before multiple rounds from the mini-Draco splattered his skull against the curb.

Chapter 8

The Dodge Challenger SRT Demon's engine was so enormously powerful that the car actually popped a wheelie when Lacey slammed her foot down on the pedal and raced off down Kostner Avenue.

They snatched off their masks. Nya put her mini-Draco on the floor in front of her black Dior sneakers and fixed her frazzled hair in the visor mirror. Her light brown eyes were red veined from crying all night and smoking blunts all morning. She hadn't put on any makeup; the darkness below her eyes betrayed her lack of sleep. Her heart was pounding out reggae beats in her chest, and her hands were tremulous, but she was more focused than ever.

She waited until they were twenty blocks away from Washington and Kostner before she turned on her phone. Which didn't take long at all. Lacey Carter was like Jimmie Johnson behind the wheel. There were three instances when Nya feared they were going to crash, but Lacey would whip the steering wheel one way and brake and get them out of the jam without so much as a graze.

The first thing Nya did was transfer $150,000 to Raven Hillman's bank account. It was the money she'd offered the stripper to give up her baby daddy, Bryce's location. She'd messaged Nya on WhatsApp saying Bryce's cousin, Jabar, was also there, and Nya had come very close to smiling when she read it.

But there would be no smiling. Not for a while. Nya's mind was set on avenging Grizzy's murder, and she was willing to spend every dollar of the millions she had in the bank to get it done.

She'd ghosted Bankroll Reese after failing to show for her performance at his nightclub, and even though he'd DM'd her early this morning, offering his condolences regarding her husband's death, she wasn't going to respond to the message. Bulletface had texted her, asking if she was okay after learning that she hadn't boarded his private jet early this morning, and she'd ghosted him too. The only people she'd spoken with were her parents, her son, and Grizzy's mother and sister, and those calls were very brief and to the point. They had killed Grizzy, she'd told them, and she wasn't going to rest until she figured out who exactly "they" were.

She hadn't told them about Bang Boy, but he was at the very top of her kill list. She went to his Instagram page, though she'd already perused it ten minutes ago. He'd posted a video someone had taken of him and his gang walking up the steps of a Gulfstream 650. They were dressed in high-end designer from head to toe, three of them carrying large Louis Vuitton duffle bags. They had five sexy young women with them, and Nya had wasted an hour studying their faces, trying to identify them. Then, Lacey had pointed out that they could play the video in front of one of the Panteon home security cameras and use the facial recognition technology to identify them, and Nya had learned that they were all Instagram models based in the Los Angeles area, women Bang Boy and his gang had likely met while gallivanting around town in their foreign cars. The facial recognition tech had also identified Bang Boy's four friends. Nya was stalking their social media pages too, and she'd already figured out where one of them hung out. His name was Faheem Waters, and he owned a sports bar in the Roseland neighborhood. His wife and son worked there. Marcus and six other Gangster Disciples were currently parked outside the building in two different SUVs.

Bang Boy's Instagram video was captioned "Back to Chicago I go," followed by an airplane emoji.

Nya could not *wait* to see the next post.

She was watching the video again when an incoming call from Bulletface came through, and her fingers were so shaky that she accidentally accepted it. The sight of him on her phone screen elicited a small gasp from Nya. Momentarily stunned, she brought one hand up to cover her gaping mouth.

Blake "Bulletface" King's eyes were as red as Nya's. There was a dense haze of smoke rising in front of his face. She could see the double-R embroidered in the headrest behind him, so she knew he was in a Rolls Royce, probably riding through Miami with Alexus "Queen A" Costilla-King seated next to him.

But then, he switched to his rear camera, and Nya gasped again as he slowly panned the camera across the fleet of snow-white Rolls Royce Cullinans, Phantoms, and Wraiths that were parked all around him.

"You're here in Chicago," she muttered incredulously.

More specifically, he was at the Highland Park mansion, parked in the circular driveway out front. Most of the men and women standing outside of the Rolls Royces — smoking thick blunts, drinking from Styrofoam cups, engaging in conversation — were MBM rap artists. Nya recognized Young Meach, Will Scrill, D. Boy, Deja, and Yonna and Lynx of the Trap Twinz duo. All of them wore an MBM pendant on one of their diamond necklaces. Seeing all of the rap superstars lingering out front of the mansion she'd been living in brought a hint of a smirk to Nya's pretty mouth.

"I ain't wanna just barge into the crib with you livin' here now," Blake said, his diamond teeth twinkling like the reflective squares on a disco ball. "I heard about what happened to your man. I'm pretty sure I know who was behind it. Where you at right now?"

"On my way there," Nya said drably. "Give me about twenty minutes. Y'all can go on in."

"A'ight. I'll be in the studio." He ended the call.

Although she was sure Blake had the keys to his own mansion, Nya turned on her other iPhone — the one she had registered in her own name — and went to the Panteon app to unlock the door electronically. She ignored the alerts Panteon had sent her concerning the arrival of the nine white Rolls Royces. She glanced over at Lacey, and it was apparent from the stunned expression on Lacey's face that she'd seen Bulletface on Nya's phone screen.

"I'll never be able to get over that," Lacey said after a time.

"Get over what?"

"The fact that you actually *know* Bulletface. You're actually signed to his record label. That shit just blows my mind." Lacey's tone was as shaky as Nya's hands, and she kept checking the rearview mirror. They were on Lake Street, near their old stomping grounds in the Austin neighborhood.

Nya began flicking her eyes around too, searching for another target. She was suspicious of everyone in her circle, but at the moment, she was too focused on revenge to contemplate the source of betrayal. It was a process, she told herself. Soon, she would find out who'd turned on Grizzy (and clearly *someone* had; there was no other way for the men who'd killed him to have known that he was in the backseat of his Ghost with the curtains drawn shut), and when she identified the traitor, she was going to drop another body.

As if reading Nya's mind, Lacey said, "You think it was Marcus, don't you?"

Nya shrugged her shoulders. "I can't see how it could've been anybody else. I mean, I know it wasn't you. We were together. The only way somebody other than Marcus could've known that Grizzy was in that backseat was if

Grizzy told them, and I highly doubt he did that. I wish I could check his phone to be sure, but... well, you know."

Lacey did know. They'd both seen Grizzy's smartphone tumble out onto the pavement as the paramedics were pulling him from the backseat. All the gunshot wounds in Grizzy's body had made Nya cringe, and she'd averted her eyes, looking down at his phone only to find that it too had suffered multiple bullet wounds.

Her eyes became teary at the memory of the many holes she'd seen in the side of Grizzy's face. She shook off the image and thumbed away the moisture, sniffled, and refocused on the street ahead.

"Ain't no tellin' who it was," Lacey said, "but I see why you'd suspect Marcus. Just know I'm with you, right or wrong. I know Marcus is my man and all, but if we havin' to fuck him around, I'm with it."

Nya gave a small nod. Truthfully, she did believe there was a high probability that Marcus had betrayed Grizzy for a slice of that $5 million, but she couldn't cross Bam off the list of potential traitors. Bam was the chief of the Dark Side TVLs, and since Bulletface was a member of the same gang, Nya felt like she couldn't trust the man she'd signed to.

She would keep an eye on all of them, and as soon as she got everything figured out, she was going on a rampage.

Chapter 9

`"Some opps just hopped out on Bryce and Jabar and hit em up. Caught em walkin' out of Raven's spot over there on Washington and Kostner. Some lil niggas over there saw the whole thing. They say two bitches jumped out of a black Challenger wearin' pink ski masks and walked down on Lord n'em. Whacked both of em."

Red Rum's mouth dropped open. A dollop of mashed potato fell from one corner of his bottom lip and landed with a soft splat on his bare gut as he stared blankly at his younger brother, waiting for him to say it was a joke.

But eighteen-year-old Keith "Blammer" Green said no such thing. He was as serious as could be, standing there by the refrigerator with one arm in a sling, half-empty pack of peanut M&M's in one hand. Blammer's pregnant girlfriend was behind him, and behind her stood three more teenage Cold Gang members.

Shaking his head, Red Rum wiped his mouth and gut with a paper towel and picked up his smartphone. He dialed Bryce's number and listened to the steady ring. When the voicemail came on, he ended the call and went to Bryce's Facebook page.

Two people had posted "R.I.P." on his page, along with several sad face emojis and prayer hands.

Red Rum, a short, heavyset man in gray, cotton, Nike shorts and white, low-top Air Force Ones, got up from the kitchen table. The youngsters moved aside as he walked from the kitchen to the living room of his small, two-bedroom apartment. It was a duplex located on Central Avenue, just across the street and two houses down from Nya's friend, Brielle's house.

Opening the venetian blinds over his living room's picture window, he looked outside, leaning a little, his eyes scanning the area around Briella's place, his bald head slowly swiveling from left to right in disbelief. He moved wrong and winced; he'd been shot through the side six weeks ago in the Keystone Avenue shooting that had killed Mikey, Derrick, and Dre, and the wound was still healing.

He was rubbing one hand over his smooth scalp, just about to move away from the window, when a black Dodge Challenger with a loudly rumbling engine turned off of Chicago Avenue and on to Central, pulling to the curb directly across the street from Brielle's house.

Jared "Red Rum" Green knew who was in the Challenger before the doors even opened, but he kept watching anyway. just to be sure.

"Blammer, go grab yo' pistol," he said when he finally turned away from the window. "That black Challenger just pulled up and parked two houses down from here. It's Lacey and Nya."

Blammer didn't budge. Neither did his three male friends.

"Fuck that," Blammer said, shaking his head in refusal. "I'm *not* fuckin' with Nya. Shorty like twenty and oh out here. Every nigga who done crossed that bad lil bitch got *whacked*. I'll be damned if I be the next one."

Red Rum glared at his younger brother. Blammer had a point but still. There would be no backing down, especially not from a fucking *woman*.

"Nigga," Red Rum said, "that lil bitch is four foot *nothin'*. The *fuck* is you scared of?! Ain't nobody invincible around this muhfucka. Somebody caught up with her man last night and shot him forty some'n times. Her lil ass can go the same way."

"And that's exactly why I'm not fuckin' with that bitch," Blammer reasoned. He walked up behind his pregnant girlfriend and put his good arm around her. "If Nya killed all these niggas *before* her husband got killed, what the fuck you think she gon' do *after* he got killed? Go ape shit, that's what, and I ain't about to be the next victim. Shit, shorty got Bulletface behind her now. That nigga a billionaire. They say Nya got like twenty million dollars. I don't want no smoke."

"That's why we just flipped to Baby T Blood Gang," said Thrax, Blammer's rail thin friend. Baby T Blood Gang was a faction of Traveling Vice Lords that operated in the area of Chicago Avenue and Trumbull. Red Rum knew that but what he *hadn't* known was that Blammer's three friends had switched gangs on him.

Red Rum started to make another attempt at convincing Blammer and his boys to ride with him, but he ultimately decided against it. Instead, he lifted his white tee shirt from the arm of the sofa and put it on to conceal the butt of the 45 caliber Smith and Wesson handgun on his hip.

"You lil niggas is bitches," he barked, snatching open his front door.

"We gon' be some alive bitches," Blammer shouted back as Red Rum stepped out onto the front porch.

Red Rum slammed the door shut behind him, and when Blammer fingered the blinds down to peek outside, Red Rum almost pulled his gun and pointed it at his nosey brother's face, but he kept his composure and watched the Challenger.

Through the windshield, he could see two young women, Lacey Carter and Nya Mixon. Lacey was holding a phone up in front of her mouth, and her lips moved as she stared across the street at Brielle's house.

Nya's squinted eyes were staring right at Red Rum.

He was tempted to pull his gun and shoot right then, but there was an old woman walking past on the sidewalk in front of his house. Her name was Miss Mason, and she knew his full name. She knew both of his parents. She was a pastor at the church his mother attended, and her youngest son was a CPD homicide detective.

So, Red Rum dug a nearly empty pack of Newport cigarettes out of his pocket and put the butt of one between his lips. He fired it up and sucked in a mouthful of smoke. Miss Mason waved at him and said to tell his mama she'd better see her in church this weekend. He nodded and said he would tell her, and Miss Mason continued down the sidewalk, moving briskly for a woman in her early seventies. The old lady clearly had somewhere to go.

When he looked at the Challenger again, he saw that both Nya and Lacey were staring back at him. Four of their friends — Brielle, Quita, Noesha, and Niecy — were walking down Brielle's porch steps, heading for a red Cadillac SUV that was parked at the curb, and every one of them had their eyes on Red Rum.

His heartbeat hastened as a rush of adrenaline surged through him. He was about to do it. Miss Mason was still on the block, but so what? He'd opened fire on his rivals right in front of the police before. Sure, certain people would be judgmental of him for shooting at a woman as small and sexy as Nya Mixon, but all the street niggas who knew her would understand. She was a menace, a nightmare, and somebody needed to put an end to her before she took out the entire Cold Gang hierarchy.

He stepped forward to look both ways, making sure there were no police in the vicinity. He looked to the right, in the direction Miss Mason was walking.

There were no police down there, just a couple of fat chicks drinking Slurpees, a fat, little toddler in a miniature Jeep, and a brown-haired mutt on a leash.

He turned his head to look to the left and saw that Nya's door was hanging open.

The pretty, little woman wore a pink ski mask on her head, a pink Barbie hoodie with a photo of actress Issa Rae printed on the chest, and tight black jeans, and she was sprinting up the sidewalk with a mini-Draco raised and aimed right at Red Rum.

He whipped the 45 from his waist just as she opened fire. He lifted the 45 just as four or five supersonic 7.62 rifle rounds drilled through his fat, round belly and pendulous man boobs. The impact was akin to being punched four or five times by a steroid abusing Mike Tyson. It knocked him backwards and sent him reeling against his closed storm doon. His eyes bulged out in panic as he suddenly realized he was unable to breathe. It felt like he was drowning in a liquid much thicker than water.

He squeezed the trigger of his pistol as he watched the masked woman rush up onto the porch steps, but his gun was aimed at the concrete floor of his porch when he did it, and the bullet simply ricocheted into the clapboard porch wall.

"I've been looking for you," Nya said, aiming the mini-Draco at his face. "Tell your boy, Sleet, I said hi."

Forty-two-year-old Jared Green glimpsed a brief flash of light, and then, there was nothing but darkness.

Chapter 10

The state-of-the-art recording studio inside the Highland Park mansion had three separate soundproof booths. The walls in each booth were padded with a noise-canceling material sourced from Elon Musk's SpaceX rocket production company. The microphones suspended from the ceilings inside the booths were plated in 24-karat gold, and when Nya and four of her girlfriends walked into the studio at a quarter past two in the afternoon, MBM rap star Young Meach (who mostly went by Y.M. nowadays) was demonstrating his clever wordplay in the booths while iconic beatmaker Tay Keith sat at the soundboard wearing headphones and vibing to the music.

Blake "Bulletface" King and a few other MBM recording artists were standing around the room, bobbing their heads to Y.M.'s hot new verse. Several of them were smoking blunts, and the room was foggy with weed smoke.

The first thing everyone looked at when Nya walked into the studio was the mini-Draco she was holding down by her side. She'd gone into her bedroom and changed into white Givenchy sweatpants and a matching tee shirt, and Quita had left out to get rid of the clothes Nya and Lacey had worn during the shootings, but the one thing Nya absolutely refused to part ways with was her mini-Draco pistol. She'd put on the diamond-studded Audemars Piguet watch Grizzy had bought her to celebrate her record deal and the $100,000 Cuban-link necklace that had her icy MBM pendant attached to it. In all honesty, she was drowning in a bottomless ocean of grief, but she wasn't about to let everyone else know it.

She handed the mini-Draco off to Noesha as her fellow MBM artists stepped forward and greeted her with warm smiles and even warmer hugs. The closest she'd ever come to meeting a celebrity before now was when she and Lacey had been front row at a Moneybagg Yo concert in early May. She'd always suspected she'd scream her head off if she ever met Bulletface in person, but she was much too shell-shocked by all that had happened since last night to offer him anything more than a barely there grin as he wrapped an arm around her and pulled her tight against his Celine tee shirt.

He smelled amazing, a lust-inducing combination of shea butter, designer cologne, and high-grade marijuana. He wasn't as tall as Grizzy, but he was tall nonetheless, and he was so *handsome*. The circular bullet scars in his face and arms added a gritty edge to his already thuggish appearance. The numerous necklaces and bracelets he wore had massive white diamonds in them. Black Twitter often compared him to Gucci Mane if Gucci had Jay-Z's money, and Nya thought that was an accurate description. Bulletface was the undisputed king of diamonds. He owned more jewelry than an Egyptian pharaoh, and he revealed another blinging pendant every couple of weeks.

Bulletface was also the king of gangsters, if ever there was such a thing. Over the years, he'd been accused of committing a long list of homicides. He'd been arrested for several of them, and his elite team of criminal defense attorneys had beaten every charge. He was the billionaire gangsta rapper all the street niggas looked up to. Nya's father had told her stories about the days when Blake had supplied Bankroll Reese's now deceased father with tons of cocaine. Those were the days when Blake had been locked all the way in with the Dark Side TVLs, the days when he'd driven around the west side of Chicago in a lime green Bugatti Veyron with a few million dollars in cash on him at all times, the days when he'd gone to war with other notorious gangsters and emerged victorious every time.

Which was why Nya was glad to have signed with his record label and why she was eager to get a word with him in private.

"Let's step out in the hallway real quick," he said; apparently, he wanted a one-on-one conversation with her as well.

She gave him a nod and walked out ahead of him, leaving her starstruck friends to mingle with the MBM rap stars.

The hallway outside the studio was enormous with white marble flooring and large, expensive paintings on the clean, white walls. There was an entertainment room across the hall. The other MBM artists were in there, shooting pool and talking while a Trap Twinz twerk anthem played from the speakers.

"I'm sorry to hear about what happened to your husband," Blake said, streaming twin jets of weed smoke from his nostrils.

"It's cool," Nya said coldly. "I killed one of them too, and three more niggas got stretched before I got here. That's four bodies in less than twenty-four hours. And I'm about to turn up some more on these fuck niggas soon as I find out who else was in that Magnum."

"Between me and you, my nigga, Bam, told me it was Johnna Broward's brother who dropped the bag on your man."

"I know. Bam was here in the mansion with us when Bang Boy called him. I'm on Bang Boy's ass too."

Nya folded her arms across her chest and glanced into the entertainment room. Lynx was bent over on one of the pool tables, shaking her fat ass while holding an open fifth of Hennessy. Lynx was one of Nya's favorite rappers. She was a bad yellow bone from Dallas with a flow that reminded Nya of Megan Thee Stallion.

When she turned back to Blake, he had his head tilted a little to one side, eyeing her like she was some sort of rare art exhibit.

"What?" Nya uncrossed her arms and planted her hands on her hips. "Why you lookin' at me like that?"

Blake laughed. "Nothin'." He glanced at his diamond flooded Patek Philippe wristwatch. "Look, I know you're grieving right now, but we need to get to this money. Focus all that pent-up aggression into the music. My brother sent me those songs you recorded. Including the single we got out now, you got eight songs we can drop now on that debut album. Which ain't bad. Look at Ice Spice and GloRilla. A lot of women drop albums with only seven or eight songs. We can do that and just relax for a lil while, give you some time to heal."

"Nah, nah," Nye said, shaking her head vehemently. "I'll record at least another eight songs for the album, and I'll do ten more for the deluxe version. My first album gotta be bussin'. Straight gang shit."

Blake's mouth widened into a beaming smile that showed all twenty of his diamond teeth. He laughed again and adjusted the crotch of his designer jeans. He had a brown Louis Vuitton bandana draped over his left shoulder. A Glock pistol with a thirty round clip jutted out from the holster under his left arm, and Nya could see the small square button on the back of the slide.

Nya's prepaid smartphone buzzed in her pocket. She took it out and saw that she'd just received a text message from Marcus.

"Was just lookin at that video on Bang Boy page and peeped the tail number on his private jet. I looked it up on the flight tracker app. It landed at Midway airport not even ten minutes ago."

Nya texted back. "Just lamp on em outside that sports bar. I got a feeling they'll be stopping by there sometime soon.

Faheem gon wanna show everybody that he knows Johnna's brother, and Bang Boy loves the spotlight."

"But what if they don't show up?"

"Then go in there and kill Faheem's wife."

She pocketed the phone and looked up at Blake, knowing that he'd seen every message she'd typed. He was still smiling, nodding his head, and biting down on the center of his bottom lip.

"They told me you was a real deal gangsta bitch," he said. "Bankroll Reese told me all the stories the day I had my assistant mail you that chain, but I had to see it for myself."

"Let's get in this studio and make some real deal gangsta *music*," Nya said, one side of her pretty mouth rising into a nefarious grin.

Young Meach had just exited the booth when Nya and Blake re-entered the studio. He gave her a hug in passing and handed her the blunt he'd been smoking, and she went in the same booth he'd just left out of, taking out her other iPhone as she stepped up to the mic and reaching up to pull it down in front of her. She put on the headphones and began reading over the lyrics to a song she'd written yesterday afternoon. It was somewhat of a love song to Grizzy, but since she wasn't feeling particularly lovey dovey at the moment (and also because she didn't want to break down crying in front of her CEO), she nixed that idea and put her phone away. She was good at freestyling; in the days since her hit single with Bulletface was released, the freestyle she'd uploaded to YouTube a few months ago had gotten over three hundred thousand views with the majority of comments showing that the listeners loved her grimy flow.

Deja and the Trap Twinz had entered the studio seconds behind Blake, and now, nearly every rap artist on MBM's roster was watching Nya from outside the booth.

Nya shut her eyes, puffed on the blunt, and coughed like an unvaccinated Covid-19 patient. She struggled to arrange her thoughts as Tay Keith turned on a drumming beat that got her to bobbing her head and mouthing a couple of silent words to get herself going.

And then, she opened her eyes and went straight in.

"MBM gang, we on top like the star on a tree
Ride through my city, AR on the seat
Walk down with that glizzy, leave scars on the street
Then I'm back in the booth to go hard on a beat
Bulletface signed me 'cause he know my reputation
I hop out and start bussin', no conversation
Tell the opps ain't no duckin', I'm hittin' faces
Yo' best bet is to stay out my situations
Cause you know I ain't goin' for none
That bulge in my Birkin, you know it's a gun
I'm up $20 million, but I want a hun'
That boy disrespects me, then I want him done..."

Nya rode the beat for almost four minutes straight, impervious to the stunned expressions on the faces of her fellow MBM artists. Most of them were staring at her with open mouthed smiles. Deja and the Trap Twinz were jumping up and down with excitement, Lynx spilling Hennessy all over her hand as the contents of her bottle sloshed around with her every leap. Blake threw his Louis Vuitton bandana in the air, gesticulating as if he'd just watched an NBA game in which his favorite athlete had scored the game-winning point. Lacey and the rest of Nya's Plush Gang Crew were equally elated, Lacey and Niecy recording video of the freestyle with their iPhones, Brielle and Noesha rocking their hips and bobbing their heads, fully enthralled by Nya's lyrical genius.

The ecstatic reactions hardly even registered in Nya's brain. The freestyle was more of an emotional release than an attempt at impressing all the people looking in at her. She was merely speaking the truth, and it only came out gangster because it *was* gangster. Chicago's gang culture was no joke, and Nya had grown up right in the thick of it. She'd gone from fighting bitches in her school years to actually killing people, and she'd become so desensitized to the violence that she could kill a man today and not even think about it tomorrow.

She exited the booth to a flurry of hugs and shouts, and she responded with the same bland grin she'd given Blake in the hallway. Physically, she was present in the recording studio, but mentally, she was elsewhere, thinking about Bang Boy and his gang and the man who'd pulled up alongside her husband's Rolls Royce Ghost and shot him dead. She figured Bang Boy had flown into Chicago simply to deliver the cash he'd promised to the killers, and part of her wondered if Marcus was going to separate from his gang to go and collect his share of that $5 million.

She was still lost in contemplation when Blake pulled her close again. He lowered his mouth to her ear and whispered, "Focus on your music. You're the breadwinner now, not just for yourself but for everybody you love. If you wanna go to war with them niggas, you need to hire some fulltime steppers and just start payin' *them* to take care of your enemies. My wife's net worth is $225 *billion*, and you wouldn't even believe me if I told you how much money we got stashed away. If Bang Boy dropped $5 million on your man, we'll drop $10 million on him. I just want you to get back in that booth and record a few more songs. Record a couple of feature verses for the MBM compilation album we got droppin' in September. I'm setting you up to make millions. Forget about the opposition for now. We got money to make."

"No, I can't do that. I'm not resting until…"

"Be quiet." He said it authoritatively. Like a boss. "Follow me."

This time, he led the way out of the studio. Nya had a 10-millimeter Glock tucked inside the front of her Savage X Fenty panties, and she adjusted it as she followed Blake up the hallway. They made three turns and were approaching the gymnasium when he stopped at a large red door marked

"Maintenance Only." There was a digital keypad next to the door. Blake typed in an eight-digit code, and there was an audible click as the locking mechanism disengaged. Blake pulled open the door, and Nya's eyes widened a little when she saw another door beyond the first one — a massive steel door with another digital keypad and a handprint identification pad right at the center of it.

Blake was too wide for Nya to see the passcode he typed in, but a few seconds later, the huge steel door buzzed with a pneumatic hiss, and Blake helped her inside before reaching back to shut the big red door.

Nya only saw him reach to shut the door in her peripheral; she could not take her eyes off the contents of the enormous walk-in safe she was standing in.

The safe room took up at least one thousand square feet of living space. Against the far back wall, there were pallets upon pallets of cellophane-wrapped cash. It was organized in four rows and stacked almost to the ceiling and was all hundred-dollar bills, by the looks of it. The metal shelves on the walls were stacked three feet high with packets of hundreds. Four gray marble tables stood parallel to each other in the center of the room, two of them piled high with bank-new packets of hundreds, the other two covered in black velvet and displaying dozens of diamond necklaces, watches, bracelets, finger rings, and earrings.

Nya walked over to one of the tables and picked up a packet of hundreds. She thumbed through it and looked around the room in amazement.

"Jesus Christ," she muttered in sheer disbelief.

"Now, do you see what I'm sayin?" Blake stood with his massive arms folded across his chest, nodding his head as if he'd won an argument. "You see those pallets back there? That's why we had to make the doorway so wide — so we could fit the heavy-duty forklifts in here. We got $200 million in hundreds on each one of those pallets. And that's forty pallets. While you do the math on that, add the $100 million we got on each one of these shelves, and the $100 million on each of these two tables. Go ahead. Go ahead. I'll wait."

Nya was thunderstruck. She was usually quick with numbers, but for some reason, she kept feeling like her calculations were off when it came to the pallets of cash she was gawking at. She calculated the numbers again and again and kept getting the same mind-shattering amount: $8 billion.

"There's no way in hell you've got over eight billion dollars in cash sitting here in this safe," she murmured incredulously. "No. Fucking. Way."

"That's just trap money, lil mama. Money we made sellin' bricks, bales, and fentanyl pills here in the Midwest over the past three or four years, laundered through a couple of banks to get rid of the old bills and bring in these new blue faces. We got a whole lot more money than Johnna. Believe that. She gave Bang Boy $100 million. If you want, I'll let you bag up $10 million right now, and you can have that nigga dead by sundown. All you gotta do is keep your mouth shut about the contents of this safe and get the fuck back in that booth."

Nya spun around on the toes of her all-white Givenchy running shoes with a full-on smile spanning the width of her stunningly attractive face — the first real smile she'd worn since her husband's murder.

"Deal," she said, extending her hand for a shake.

Blake took her hand in his, and they shook on it.

Chapter 11

Alaina White was curled up on the sofa in her Country Club Hills townhouse, incessantly patting her wet eyes with a Kleenex tissue, shaking and sobbing uncontrollably as the crippling reality of her dear brother, Lejon's murder hit her like a ton of bricks.

She could see clearly now. Lejon had been right all along. He'd told her that her old friend, Johnna Broward, was a snake. He'd told her that Johnna had stolen $23 million of their father, Willie White's drug money from the man Alaina had always called Uncle Butch and used it to start Panteon Technologies, and he'd urged her to stop working as Johnna's personal assistant. They'd actually had a falling out over it at his engagement party when he'd wired their mother, Ne-Ne, $2 million and told them to leave town for the next few weeks.

That was the same night their father was stabbed to death in the federal prison he and Johnna's brother, Bang Boy, were housed in. Lejon had told her that he believed Bang Boy was behind the murder, but she hadn't believed him. He'd sent her a screenshot of a bank transaction showing that Bang Boy had paid the mother of another prisoner $1 million on the very same day their father was murdered, and she still hadn't believed him. Johnna Broward was one of Alaina's closest friends, one of the girls she'd known since they were kids on the far southside of Chicago, and she'd honestly believed that Lejon had only been jealous of Johnna and

Bang Boy because Johnna had made it out of the hood to become the billionaire CEO of Panteon Technologies. It wasn't until Monday afternoon at their father's funeral that Lejon had shown Alaina his own bank statement, revealing that Johnna had wired him $23 million. That was when she actually started believing him. She'd called and asked Johnna about it, and Johnna had denied the whole thing, which had *really* made Alaina believe her older brother.

Last night, Alaina had a received a voicemail from Lejon.

Just wanted to call and check in with you, let you know I'm on my way to The Visionary Lounge for Nya's first show. I, uhhh... I love you, sis. I know you don't believe me about the whole thing with Johnna and Bang Boy but please be alert when you go outside. Bang Boy just upped the stakes in a major way. He put some millions on my head, and ain't no tellin' who around and will snake me for that kinda money. If anything happens, tell Mama and Kamari I said I love em, and whenever y'all need som money, just ask Nya.

Alaina shuddered at the memory of the voicemail. Never in all her twenty-nine years had Lejon ever called to "check in" with her. Some part of him had known that death was lurking just around the corner when he made that call, and he'd been murdered just a few minutes later.

Throwing back her Chanel blanket, Alaina reached for her elaborately etched bottle of Muse De Miraval Rosé wine and refilled her crystal wine glass. She was watching the four o'clock news on her eighty-inch smart TV, trying to see if there were any updates about Lejon's murder. The news anchor had mentioned it at the beginning of the broadcast, but then, he'd moved on to the breaking news of a double homicide that had just taken place on Washington and Kastner and another murder that went down minutes later on Central Avenue.

Alaina shook her head and drank her wine. Over the past few months, there had been a drastic escalation in gun violence on Chicago's west side, but not once had Alaina expected her own brother would be the next victim. Alaina was a successful business owner now, with two fast food restaurants and a cleaning service she owned in full, but she still had friends and family members who were knee deep in the streets, and she'd heard from multiple people that Lejon's wife was responsible for most of the murders. As much as Alaina believed in the Lord, she couldn't help hoping that at least one of the three west side murders that had taken place today was done in retaliation for her brother's murder.

And judging from the comments on Nya's social media, police description of the suspect vehicle in the Central Avenue murder — a matte black Dodge Challenger SRT Demon that looked a lot like the one Lejon had bought back in February — the killer was undoubtedly Nya Mixon.

Alaina wasn't really all that surprised. Nya had told her early this morning that she was going to find out who killed Lejon and put an end to them, and she had sounded deathly serious when she said it.

There was a sudden crash in the kitchen, a shattering of glass. Alaina's head shot up and turned to look over the rear of her beige leather sofa just as her five-year-old daughter, Ellen, came running out of the kitchen like a crook on the lam.

"It was Jayden!" Ellen shouted, blaming the incident on her ten-month-old baby brother though he was spending the summer with his father way out in Detroit.

"Get your little bad ass in your room and stay there!" Alaina shouted back, shaking her head as she got up and slipped her feet into her furry, white, Chanel slippers.

Her phone buzzed on her cocktail table. She looked at the phone screen, saw that it was Ellen's deadbeat father, Dayquan, calling, and started to ignore it. But then, she remembered that Dayquan's cousin, Butter, was one of the Black P. Stones who'd been hanging out with Bang Boy ever since he got out of federal prison, so she went ahead and answered the call as she ventured into the kitchen to investigate the crash.

"What do you want, Quan?" She said it in a drab, despondent tone of voice; she was both sad over Lejon's death and exasperated by Dayquan's failure as a father.

"I just wanted to call and say sorry to hear about what happened to your bro. On Stone, you know that was my nigga."

Alaina rolled her eyes, put the call on speaker, and placed her iPhone on the granite counter, so she could grab the broom and start sweeping up the broken glass and the chocolate chip cookies that had scattered across the floor when the cookie jar shattered.

"Y'all heard anything yet?" Quan asked.

No, but I bet you did, Alaina thought to herself.

"Just that he was in the back of his Rolls Royce when he got shot," she said, sweeping. "They FaceTimed my mama from the morgue, so she could identify the body. She's fucked up over that shit."

"Man, that's crazy." Quan went silent for a moment. There was a G Herbo song playing in the background, and Alaina could hear a group of men in conversation. Then, Quan lowered his voice and said, "Look, I ain't supposed to tell this, so don't tell *nobody*, alright?" Quan spoke in a whisper. "Bang Boy just paid some nigga named Puncho for the hit. Look, I know you ain't tryna hear this, but I think it was y'all cousin, Marcus, who set Grizzy up. Puncho said it was a nigga with Grizzy when the whole shit went down. That's why they only shot up the backseat. Marcus was in the driver's seat, wasn't he?"

Alaina's head dropped. So did her lower jaw. "Wait, wait, wait. Give me one second." She hurriedly swept the glass and cookies onto the dustpan and dumped it in the trash, then she scooped up her phone and rushed back to the living room. She grabbed her glass of Rosé and finished it off in two long gulps. "Okay. Okay, tell me that again."

"Man, you heard me," Quan said. "I think it was your cousin. We at this big ass Airbnb mansion right now, down the road from that house Bulletface bought from Michael Jordan, but they about to hop back on the jet and fly to New York. Guess they gotta slide on some bitch who sued Johnna about some'n."

"Hm." Alaina nodded her head thoughtfully. "Thank you. I was definitely wondering who told them my brother was back there."

"It's the least I could do. Can I slide on you? I ain't askin' for no money this time. Butter just gave me twenty racks to get back on my feet. I can give you that thousand dollars I borrowed from you last month, and I got a band for my daughter too."

Alaina thought it over. Quan was a deadbeat, but he had some good dick, and that was exactly what she needed. Plus, he'd just given her some important details about her brother's murder. He deserved a reward for that.

"Yeah," she said finally. "Come on over. You can keep your money. Ellie's well taken care of. Just bring some weed and some condoms."

Quan was chuckling as Alaina hung up on him. She poured the remainder of her three-hundred-dollar Rosé in her wine glass and sat thinking for a minute. Then, she raised her phone, typed out a message to Nya, and smiled wickedly as she pressed send.

Chapter 12

"So," Johnna asked, twirling a dozen strings of noodle around her fork, "what was so urgent that you would fly all the way from Miami Beach just to have a chat with little old me?"

Alexus Costilla didn't answer immediately. She was too busy admiring the ten-foot-wide Julian Schnabel painting that hovered over the dining room. They were inside the Torrisi Bar and Restaurant on Manhattan's Lower East Side. Johnna had ordered the capellini with lobster, which had a Cantonese flavor to it thanks to the ginger and scallion cooked into the noodles. Alexus had settled for a raviolini with pieces of prawn perfectly cooked inside a delicate pasta drizzled in an olive oil and saffron sauce.

This was Johnna's first time ever dining at the Michelin-starred restaurant, but apparently, it was the place to be for A-list celebrities. She'd seen Meryl Streep hanging out at the bar a few minutes before Alexus arrived in her sparkling white fleet of Cadillac Escalades. Ben Stiller and Adam Sandler were also in the building. Though, of course, there was no one on Earth richer and more famous than Alexus Costilla. There were numerous people staring at their table, beaming, pointing, sneaking photos. The five huge Mexican men in flawless white business suits, who'd accompanied Alexus into the restaurant, were already hard at work, blocking the smartphone cameras with their oversized hands and whispering sternly to the transgressors.

"You've got a rat on your hands," Alexus said, taking a modest bite of her raviolini as she chewed and swallowed. She covered her mouth with a napkin, watching Johnna with those piercing green eyes of hers. She wore a skintight, white, sequined dress that was see-through in places, white, open toe Giuseppe Zanetti heels, a diamond Vacherin Constantin watch on her wrist. She wore no other jewelry besides her gigantic, twenty-carat, white diamond wedding ring.

"What do you mean a rat?" Johnna asked.

"Diana Caldwell. The FBI has scheduled a meeting with her regarding that $23 million you allegedly used to get Panteon off the ground. She was asked to come in today, but she insisted on waiting until tomorrow morning. Said she wants to sit her son down and tell him what's going on first."

Johnna became thoughtfully silent. She dug ravenously into her lobster, eating her meal on autopilot while, in her mind, she teleported herself into the FBI interrogation room where Diana Martin-Caldwell would be sitting sometime tomorrow morning. She imagined it as being a large, square room with seamless white walls and a rectangular, wooden table right in the middle of the tiled floor. There would be a long, two-way mirror embedded in the wall, behind which senior FBI officials would stand, watching Diana as she spilled her guts to some rookie agent, giving them all the information they'd need to send Johnna away to federal prison and quite possibly bankrupt Panteon Technologies.

She shot a quick glance at her own diamond watch — a Patek Philippe "Aquanaut Annual Calendar" — for the time. 5:45 p.m. If Bang Boy stuck to his flight schedule, he and his gang would be touching down in New York exactly three hours from now.

Tip had given Johnna the address to Diana's son's home in Queens. The plan was essentially set. Bang Boy would send one or two of his boys over there to sit and wait for someone to either enter or exit the house, and then, they would force them inside at gunpoint, locate Diana, and put a bullet through her head.

"This is a *deathly* serious matter," Alexus said, still covering her mouth with the napkin, though she hadn't taken a bite in several minutes. "I have a lot of money tied up in your company, and if I dump those stocks now, they'll be investigating me for insider trading right after they indict you."

"I know, I know," said Johnna. She over-chewed her lobster to buy time. Alexus wanted answers now, but Johnna needed more time to think.

One thing was certain. Johnna owed a lot of her business' success to Queen A. If Alexus had never livestreamed video on TikTok and Instagram, showing the moment she purchased a billion dollars' worth of Panteon stocks following the now infamous Panteon shooting, millions of other investors would never have followed suit, and Johnna's net worth wouldn't have quadrupled overnight.

But the fact remained that Alexus' initial billion-dollar investment was now worth $4.3 billion. It had increased her net worth to $225 billion. So, Johnna felt like they'd done each other a favor.

"I'm on top of it," she said after a moment. "I have my people on it. They'll talk with her... before tomorrow."

The way Alexus was glaring at her — head tilted forward a few degrees, green eyes asquint — reminded Johnna of the enormous snake she'd seen in a Harry Potter movie. Lord Voldemort in the form of a deadly serpent. Momentarily frightened, she averted her gaze to the table where her boyfriend, Elijah, and Tip were seated alongside her two big, Black bodyguards.

"If I lose four billion dollars," Alexus hissed, throwing down her napkin as she stood to leave, "somebody's going to lose their goddamn head!"

She spun around and departed the restaurant with Bojo, her giant head of security, leading the way, and Johnna stared after her until she was driven away in one of the pearly white Escalades.

Johnna didn't realize she'd been holding her breath until she finally exhaled in relief. She squeezed her eyes shut and breathed, and when she opened her eyes a moment later, Tip was settling into the chair Alexus had vacated.

"What was all that about?" Tip asked, folding her arms across her chest.

"It's Diana. She's supposed to be meeting with the FBI sometime tomorrow morning. Mike must have told her what Butch told him about me stealing that money. If she corroborates the statement that was made by Butch's wife when she filed that missing person's report, the Feds will indict me."

"In that case," Tip said, checking her iPhone for the time, "let's hope your brother gets here in time to silence that bitch."

Chapter 13

Shanelle Boatman had absolutely no gag reflex. Her head rose and fell quite rapidly as she slurped Bang Boy's lengthy, black erection in and out of her throat. He sat back against the headrest in the backseat of the Audi Q5 with his eyes shut and one hand roaming the valley of his lady's arched back, reveling in the moment.

Like the majority of the country, the great city of Chicago was baking beneath a heat dome that had today's temperatures hovering around ninety-seven degrees. The humidity made it much worse, but the cool air flowing through the electric SUV mitigated the heat, making it much more bearable.

Shanelle was a federal corrections officer Bang Boy had met during his nineteen-year stint in federal prison. She'd accepted a "bribe" to bring him a package of drugs several months ago, and since then, he'd given her an additional $650,000, which included the $500,000 he wired her when he was released from prison nine days ago. She lived with her children in a spacious suburban home just outside of Terre Haute, Indiana, but she'd quit her job as a C.O. and traveled to Chicago to oversee the construction of Bang Boy's south side nightclub. She'd rented a 14,500 square foot, Spanish style mansion from Airbnb for the teeth clenching price of $4,500 per week, a bill that Bang Boy had voluntarily footed, along with the cost of the Audi SUV and round the clock maid service.

In Bang Boy's opinion, every dollar he spent on Shanelle was more than worth it. Born and raised in Decatur, Georgia, she was a brown hued stunner in six-inch, Gucci stilettos and a two tone, red, summer dress by the same high-end designer. There were some extensions in her long mop of braids, and a few extra layers of Fenty cosmetics on her gorgeous visage, but the rest of her 57.7" frame was all natural, everything from her 34C breasts to her twenty-three-inch waist and forty-five-inch hips. She was a stallion like Megan, a queen like Nicki, and although Bang Boy knew there was no way he was going to be faithful to her after having served nineteen years in prison, he didn't see himself ever letting her out of his life.

The Audi truck was parked in the carport next to the Highland Park mansion. There were two black Mercedes Benz Sprinter vans parked just ahead of the Audi, and all five passengers of one Sprinter had piled into the second Sprinter with five other passengers, the women seated on the laps of the men, exotic weed smoke trapped inside the luxury van from the corpulent blunts they were smoking.

Bang Boy stole a glance at his diamond watch. He still had an hour before his sister's private jet was scheduled to take to the skies. There was plenty of time to finish getting his dick sucked.

It didn't take Shanelle very long to suck a geyser of semen out of him. Her soft, wet lips clung to his shaft, her tongue licking all over his engorged cockhead as her head moved up and down with piston-like speeds, and when his ejaculate began to spout out of him, her head went all the way down. She sealed her lips around the base of his shaft, burying the full length of him in her throat and swallowing greedily.

Finally, after twelve long minutes of fellating him, Shanelle removed her lips from his flaccid penis and tucked it back inside his Gucci underwear.

"I'll drive you to the airport," she said, using her smartphone's front camera as a mirror and applying a fresh coat of Fenty gloss to her lips. "We need to hash out a couple of things regarding the size of the female restrooms at El Rukn."

"What about em?"

"They're not large enough. I've gone over the blueprints twenty or thirty times, and I just don't feel right about those female restrooms. I know you've been gone a while, but things have changed out here. Nowadays, restrooms are essentially photo booths that women use not only to take selfies but also to fraternize with each other. We need space, and for a nightclub with three different levels and a restaurant on the roof, your architects set aside very little of that 11,000-square-feet of space for your female clientele."

"Then call and tell him," Bang Boy said, lighting a Newport cigarette as Shanelle pushed open the rear passenger's side door and ran around to the driver door. He understood her haste; the sweltering heat that rolled in was suffocating. When she got in the driver's seat, he said, "They should be listening to you anyway. I put you in charge of the whole El Rukn project. If they ain't tryna hear what you gotta say, fire whoever's in charge and hire somebody else. Simple as that."

Shanelle gave no reply, but the winning smile that graced her peanut butter brown visage spoke volumes.

Bang Boy took out his iPhone and sent a text to his boy, X-Man. A few seconds later, the Sprinter van's sliding door rolled open, and a bunch of red-eyed money leeches spilled out of it. It was Mondré, X-Man, Faheem, Butter, Dayquan, and the five bad bitches who'd accompanied them from Los Angeles. Half of them slipped into the second Sprinter van, and the rest of them returned to their seats in the first one. The engines came alive a moment later, and the two Sprinter vans led the way down the flower lined driveway.

"You need to give up those cigarettes," Shanelle said, lowering his window an inch and pressing a button to open the huge oak gate at the end of the driveway. "After nineteen years behind bars, you'd think quitting would be a cake walk."

"I did quit. Then, you brought me that package of tobacco, and I started right back up again."

"Oh, sure, blame it on me." Shanelle threw her braids to one shoulder and rolled her neck and sucked her teeth. She was a paragon Black female beauty, and she was confident enough to walk boldly in her honey brown melanated skin.

As much as Bang Boy hated to admit it, he'd caught a couple of feelings fucking around with Shanelle. It wasn't love, but it was something in that neighborhood. He took great pride in splurging on her because he knew that financial security meant a lot to a sweet, southern belle from humble beginnings. He'd purchased dozens of high-end designer outfits and handbags and had them mailed overnight to the Highland Park mansion. He'd hired two maids to help her manage the massive living space and an au pair to help out with her children in Terre Haute. He'd put her in charge of his El Rukn nightclub project for which he'd set aside $9.4 million. He'd fucked seven other women since he was released from federal prison, but none of them were as important to him as Shanelle Boatman.

He had his eyes on her as they cruised out of the gate and onto Clearview Lane. They rode past multi-million-dollar homes with huge rolling lawns and large backyard swimming pools.

Bang Boy picked up his iPhone when it buzzed with an incoming text message from Johnna.

"I hope you're still on schedule," it read.

A smirk formed on the right side of Bang Boy's mouth. He found humor in the irony that Johnna's notoriously bossy attitude — the trait that had driven their mother half-crazy when Johnna was a kid — had ultimately led to their family's immense wealth.

He replied to the text while Shanelle rapped along to the Big Latto song she'd just turned on, and when he looked up from his phone, puffing on his Newport, he gazed ahead at the back of the Sprinter van they were tailing and smiled. This was the life. He'd come home to $100 million and a down ass, Black woman who never hesitated to assist him in rebuilding his life. He had a Ferrari truck parked outside his California mansion, and he was contemplating the purchase of a three-million-dollar Bugatti Veyron. His mother and two youngest sisters, Johnesha and Johnetta, were just as wealthy as he was with numerous homes and businesses to their names. He took great pride in knowing that he'd successfully orchestrated the takeover of Willie White's engine empire. He'd directed Johnna to track down Butch Gibbs and steal the drug money from him, and she'd turned it into legitimate billions. He'd had a falling out with Willie in prison, and a million dollars was all it had taken to get a few members of the Aryan Brotherhood to murder Willie in cold blood. Back in 2002, Bang Boy and Willie's son, Grizzy, had gone to war, and they'd both lost several friends in the ensuing battles of gunfire, but now, Grizzy was dead too, shot to death by some Vice Lord named Puncho and his nephew, Pistol, the latter of whom had died in the shooting.

Puncho had arrived at Shanelle's rented home with a deep gash on the left side of his jaw. It was a graze wound, he'd explained. One of the bullets that ended his nephew's life had cut a path in his rugged brown face. He'd come alone, in a beat-to-shit Ford Fusion, and he'd left with five heavy Louis Vuitton duffle bags lined up in his trunk. Bang Boy had thought to ask him who in Grizzy's circle had betrayed him for a share of that $5 million, but the grief he'd discerned in Puncho's red-rimmed eyes dissuaded him from speaking. And besides, that was a piece of information he didn't really need. All that mattered was his enemies were no longer breathing. There was an ongoing rumor that Grizzy's sexy little girlfriend — the bad ass redbone whose hot new song with Bulletface was rapidly taking over the airwaves — was a real deal gangsta bitch who'd slain every single one of her rivals, but Bang Boy wasn't worried about it. He was a seasoned killer, a veteran in the streets of Chicago who'd used his money to defeat his opps. He was far too wealthy to be concerned about some female rapper. If it came down to it, he'd drop a bag on her head next, and she'd get buried right next to her husband. It was as simple as that.

"What the hell?" Shanelle muttered as she suddenly stepped down on the brake pedal, jarring Bang Boy from his reverie.

The Sprinter van in front of them had come to an abrupt stop right in the middle of a residential street in a less swanky section of Highland Park. Two white women in sports bras and leggings were jogging past one side of the street. An Arab man was watering a bed of flowers in front of his two-story home. On the opposite side of the street, a cute, white, female teenager was walking a small black chihuahua on a leash.

"Why in the hell would they just stop right here?" Shanelle asked.

Bang Boy shrugged his shoulders, lowered his window, and flicked his cigarette butt out the window as he stuck his head out to see what was going on.

A white Buick SUV had swerved over from the oncoming lane and stopped right in front of the leading Sprinter van. So had a slime green Dodge Charger Hellcat. The doors were just swinging open, the passengers emerging with black ski masks on their heads and Glocks and Dracos in their gloved hands.

"Shit!" Bang Boy exclaimed, dipping his head back inside the Audi and turning to Shanelle with his eyes agape. "Back up, back up, back up! It's a hit!"

Shanelle threw the Q5 into reverse just as the gunfire erupted. The gunmen hit the Sprinter vans from both sides, and all Bang Boy could do was watch as Shanelle stomped down on the gas pedal, launching them backwards. He had a

Glock pistol on his hip, but there was no sense in opening fire through the front windshield and making himself a target. The Glocks that the gunmen were firing were modified with switches, essentially making them machine guns. Bang Boy would be lucky to squeeze off two or three shots before a hundred or more rounds came raining through the Audi, so all he did was pull the Glock from his waist and hold it tight in his hand as Shanelle spun them around like a professional stunt driver and sped off.

"Oh, Jesus," Shanelle muttered, wincing against the stentorian rattle of gunfire. She ducked her head low in front of the wood grain of her steering wheel as the ominously silent electric engine propelled them forward.

Bang Boy swung around in his seat, his heart making a speed bag of his ribcage as he watched what was likely the deaths of at least one or two of his closest friends and quite possibly all four of them.

The five California women were in equal danger, but Bang Boy didn't waste a single thought on the consideration of their well-being. Mondré, X-Man, Faheem, and Butter had given their entire lives to the Almighty Black P. Stone Nation; the Cali girls had only given out or swallowed a couple of orgasms, a couple of cum shots. Bang Boy's gang meant more to him than anything.

Which was why his eyes filled with tears as Shanelle slowed the Audi from eighty-four miles per hour and rounded a corner nearly on two wheels.

"On Chief Malik," he swore, tightening his fingers around the handle of his Clock pistol, "I'm on demon time from here on out. Whoever did that just awakened a monster. Fuck New York. I'm stayin' right here in the city. If these niggas want a war, that's exactly what the fuck I'ma give em."

Chapter 14

Nya Mixon was on a roll.

She'd recorded fourteen new songs and nine feature verses in just under four hours. Bulletface had called in some favors, and two of Nya's favorite rappers — Cardi B and Lil Baby — had sent over verses that would be added to *No More Motion*, a song Nya had written just three days ago. Young Meach, Bulletface, D-Bay, and the Trap Twinz had all jumped on her newly created drill tracks.

In between recording sessions, Nya would leave out of the studio and sashay across the hall to the entertainment room, where she and her gang of gangsta girls would get down to business.

During Nya's first break from recording, she'd loaded a Louis Vuitton briefcase with two million dollars in bank-new hundreds and opened it on one of the pool tables. $300,000 had gone to Shaquita Hales, who Nya sent to the Gucci store to buy up every purse they had on display. She set aside a million dollars to pay her debts; she'd owed Grizzy's sister, Alaina, half a million for sharing Bang Boy's location, and the other $500,000 went to Grizzy's gang of Gangster Disciples for carrying out the hit. The remaining $700,000 had gone to Quita, Lacey, Brielle, Niecy, and Noesha, not only to reward them for aiding her in committing a brazen quadruple murder a little over a week ago but also because they were the five bad bitches she'd been hanging with for years, and she wanted them to be just as fly as she was on social media, especially since she knew that all her enemies were likely watching them just as closely as they were watching her.

During the second break from recording, Nya squandered fifteen minutes sitting on the side of the pool table, ordering a diamond-encrusted "Grizzy Gang" pendant from Zo Frost's custom jewelry website while her friends, Quita and Niecy, delivered the cash to Alaina and Marcus in a white, four-door Bugatti Galibier from Bulletface's exotic car collection.

And now, on her third break from recording, Nya stood watching MTN News on a ninety-inch television toward the rear of the entertainment room, where a fully stocked wet bar sat alongside a trio of long, white, leather sofas. The news anchor was describing a deadly shooting that had just taken place eight blocks from Blake's extravagant two and a half-story mansion. Two Mercedes Benz Sprinter vans had been riddled with bullets. Six dead, four more critically injured. Some teenage dog walker had also taken a bullet. There was helicopter video showing the Sprinter vans from above. Their windshields were destroyed, the exterior siding destroyed. The exterior siding was heavily packed with bullet holes, and more than a hundred yellow evidence markers littered the street in front of the lead van. The evidence markers had been placed next to the spent shell casings. A blue tent was set up about twenty feet from the crime scene; Nya figured the dead bodies were tucked away in there. Both the Chicago Police Department and the FBI were on scene, securing and canvassing the area, speaking with eyewitnesses.

Nya stared fixedly at the newscast, puffing on the blunt someone had just passed her without even looking at it, anxiously awaiting confirmation of Johnny Broward's death. She'd refilled the Louis Vuitton suitcase with another $2 million of Blake's drug money. Quita, Niecy, and Noesha had returned from a Gold Coast shopping spree with dozens of shopping bags from Dior, Fendi, Gucci, Chanel, and fifty other high-end designers. Lacey and Brielle were at a luxury car dealership, filling out the necessary paperwork to lease two Bentley Bantayans. Nya was in a dark space mentally, but seeing her friends blow through a lot of the cash she'd given them brightened her spirits a little.

Someone ripped the blunt from between her thumb and forefinger. She looked over and saw that it was Noesha "Nu-Nu" Long, the green-eyed yellow bone whose slender waist and bountiful backside turned heads everywhere she went.

"Now you know you don't need to be smoking," Nu-Nu said with a long blink and gentle sway of the neck. "At least not until you take that pregnancy test. You might have a baby growing in there."

Nya looked into Nu-Nu's captivating eyes for a long moment. Like Niecy and Quita, she wore a diamond Cuban-link necklace with a fat diamond "PLUSH GANG" pendant resting between her boobs. A diamond Cartier watch sparkled on her wrist. Her cleavage-bearing Chanel top was white with orange double-Cs all over it, and her orange leather Chanel skirt embraced her fat, round globe of an ass like a latex glove. Her wig was Beyoncé-blond, and it fell down around her gorgeous face in a razor-straight bob. She brought the blunt to her glossy pink lips and toked on it.

"Why haven't you taken that test anyway?!" Nu-Nu asked, circulating the smoke from her mouth to her nose. "I mean, you missed your period right after Grizzy dicked you down in the Bahamas, and you said y'all did it without a condom."

"I know." Nya folded her arms across her chest and sighed. "Honestly, I was thinking about an abortion. I had just signed a record deal, and I have one son that I haven't even been raising. Plus, you know... I'm too deep into the streets. Things changed when I met Grizzy. Too many people have lost their lives for me to turn back now."

Nu-Nu was shaking her pretty head. Behind her, Niecy was recording video of Quita twerking in front of all their designer shopping bags. Quita had the fattest ass in the crew, which explained why the pecan-brown New Orleans native had more social media followers than everyone but Nya. She wore a Fendi tube top with matching booty shorts that were about two sizes too small and seven-inch Louboutin heels.

"I don't think you should get an abortion," Nu-Nu said, after a time. She was nibbling at her bottom lip. She shook her head a second time. "Especially not after what happened to Grizzy. I know y'all had just met in May and your relationship moved kinda fast, but that man loved you with all his heart, and I know you loved him the same way."

"Always will," Nya murmured as she thought of the three unopened pregnancy tests she'd stashed away in her nightstand. Lacey had purchased them two days ago, and Nya hadn't looked at them since. She was procrastinating. Delaying the inevitable.

As if reading Nya's mind, Nu-Nu placed a supportive hand on Nya's shoulder and said, "Just do it, okay? Take the goddamn test. You've got nothing to lose and everything to gain, and you know we'll be right here with you no matter what."

When Nya hesitated, Nu-Nu turned to her sister, Niecy, for assistance, and suddenly, Nya was escorted out of the entertainment room with Nu-Nu's hands on the back of her shoulders and Niecy's hand wrapped tight around her wrist. Quita was mindful enough to scoop up the cash-filled briefcase on the way out.

Nya laughed and rolled her eyes as she was led through the hallway and into the bedroom of her dreams. The elaborate master's suite had four interconnecting sections with white silk-embroidered panels in the dressing chamber, plate-brass doors between the bedroom and bathroom, and a huge bathtub sculpted from a single block of Carrara marble. The massive two-story walk-in closet was a fashion lover's paradise with rows and racks of obnoxiously high-priced women's clothing in Nya's diminutive size on one side and obnoxiously high-priced men's clothing in Grizzy's size taking up the other side.

As her close friends freed her from their grasps, Nya sauntered around the Grand Vividus bed she'd been sleeping in lately, a handcrafted masterpiece designed by master craftsman Ferris Rafauli. The spacious bed was the bedroom's centerpiece, an enormous box of softness draped in sumptuous white Louis Vuitton linen. White leather upholstering on the headboard displayed the same signs and symbols as the white fur comforter. Even the white fur area rugs flanking the bed and the nine-foot curtains over the floor-to-ceiling wall of windows were Louis Vuitton.

Nya fought off the memories of all the intimate moments she and Grizzy had shared in the $55,000 bed. Opening the top drawer in her nightstand, she listened to the distant chatter of the other MBM artists. She'd checked the Panteon cameras from her iPhone ten minutes ago and found that most of Blake's entourage of millionaire rap stars were gathered around the sixty-five-foot indoor swimming pool.

It was just up the hall from the master bedroom suite.

"Nuh uh. Come on," Niecy said from the closet doorway. She looked almost identical to her sister, Nu-Nu, only she was a bit taller and more petite. She had her hands resting on the hips of her see-through Balenciaga dress, and she was staring right at Nya as Nya stood holding the boxed pregnancy tests in her small fists.

"I'm coming," Nye said with an overly dramatic sigh. She lowered her head sheepishly and walked toward her closet, thinking up another hot hook for a song and thinking about the text message she'd received from her father saying he'd found a nice home for sale in Mesa, Arizona.

Thinking about everything but Lejon "Grizzy" White.

Keeping him out of her mind had been easy in the recording booth, but now, it was rapidly becoming more and more difficult to ignore. She could smell him; his distinctive Gucci cologne invaded her nasal passage like a wave of Russian soldiers crossing Ukraine's southern border. But it wasn't until she actually entered the walk-in closet and glanced at his designer wardrobe that his absence really hit her.

The single article of clothing that struck a chord in Nya's grief-stricken heart was a black designer shirt with Dior printed all over it in red lettering. It was the shirt Grizzy was wearing when she first laid eyes on him. When Mikey and Derrick of the Cold Gang faction of Conservative Vice Lords carjacked him for his brand-new red Cadillac Escalade ESV right in the middle of Chicago Avenue. Nya and Lacey had been standing there when he was forced out of the SUV at gunpoint. He'd walked up to Nya and offered her a hundred-dollar bill to use her phone and five grand for the address to where he could find the carjackers, and she drove him to their block where he'd hopped out on them with a modified Glock and that black-and-red Dior shirt tied around his handsome black face.

Nya's vision became blurry with tears. Her knees grew weak, and she buckled two feet away from her open bathroom door. Niecy hooked one slender forearm under Nya's armpit and kept her from hitting the heated marble floor. Quita and Nu-Nu were on Nya an instant later, holding her up as she pressed her face into the crock of Niecy's neck and cried her eyes out.

A number of disturbing images flashed across Nya's mind at once. The two black handguns with high-capacity magazines sticking out of that purple Dodge Magnum, fire erupting from the barrels. The fleeting glimpse of Grizzy's bullet-riddled body she'd seen when Marcus screeched to a stop in front of the hospital door and snatched open the swiss-cheesed rear door. The grisly sight of blood and brain matter exploding out of Bryce's head as she stood over him, firing again and again.

"I hate it," Nya said, her voice muffled against Niecy's shoulder "Why did they have to kill Grizzy!? Why?!"

Niecy squeezed her tighter. So did Nu-Nu and Quita. It was the support Nya desperately needed. They held her in their arms for a long while, rubbing her back and shoulders, massaging her nape neck as she was overtaken by a fit of wracking sobs. They murmured consoling words. Quita phoned Brielle for emotional backup; it was an all hands on deck situation.

"Bri, I'ma need you and Lacey to get over here like asap," Quita said, instinctively fixing Nya's hair. She was the member of the crew who could do hair better than most professional hairstylists in their west side neighborhood.

"Why? What's poppin"?" Brielle asked.

"Sis needs us. It's Ny-Ny," Quita said, using the nickname she'd coined four years ago. "She's going through it over Grizzy. We need the whole gang over here."

"Okay, let me try and get Lacey. We're on Seventy-first and Rhodes with Marcus and his niggas. She wanted to pull up on dumbass stuntin' shit in these Bentley trucks, but ain't no fun to be had over here. Everybody strapped up and mean-muggin'. You know they just hit up the niggas who put money on Grizzy's head, and now they're callin' niggas from out' west, tryna figure out who Lil Pistol was related to. All we know so far is that it's an Undertaker Vice Lord from somewhere on Cicero."

The news of the dead shooter's identity was the catalyst for Nya's speedy emotional recovery. She sniffled twice and wiped her face. The strength returned to her knees. She released a strong sigh and forced herself to regain her composure.

"They don't need to come back over here," Nya said, tying her hair back in a quick ponytail. "Tell Marcus and his boys I got another half a million on the chief of the Undertakers over there on Cicero, and I got a whole two million on whoever the other shooter is."

Chapter 15

$140,995.00

That was the amount of money Marcus White had paid for his factory-new Mercedes Benz EQS 580 4Matic SUV, the first battery-driven model in Benz's sport utility category. It was the inside of the luxury SUV that had sold Marcus on buying it: the cutting-edge HEPA filtered interior in the seven-passenger EQS Family hauler. The dash looked like it was lifted from the set of *Black Panthers* with a state-of-the-art fifty-six-inch MBUX hyperscreen complemented by the augmented-reality heads-up display that showed a 3D representation of directions and other pertinent intel. Add the subtle infusion of fragrance and the robust Dolby Atmos sound system, which immersed passengers in three hundred sixty degrees of sound, and the cumulative cabin experience was unlike anything else Marcus had ever driven.

He was reclined in the driver's seat with a Styrofoam cup in one hand and the palm of his other hand resting on the back of Lacey's gracefully bobbing head. He'd mixed eight ounces of Wockhardt promethazine and codeine syrup with peach-flavored Crush soda and topped it off with six ice cubes - one for each point of the Loungster Disciples' six-pointed star.

Marcus was parked in the alleyway on 71st and Rhodes. Lacey and Brielle's two black Bentley Bentaygas were lined behind his sleek blue Mercedes SUV. There were other vehicles positioned at both ends of the alley and on the street out front. Blacked-out Dodge Challenger Hellcats and Jeep Grand Cherokee Trailhawks. The men who'd arrived in those vehicles were all outstanding members of the Gangster Disciple Rellion Nation, and every one of them wore shirts and other articles of clothing with *R.I.P. Lejon "Grizzy" White* airbrushed above a photo of Grizzy and Nya posing next to the black Rolls Royce Ghost that Grizzy was seated in when he lost his life.

The grief was difficult to accept. Marcus had grown up under Grizzy's tutelage, learning everything from how to tie his shoes and indent a paragraph when he was just a kid to how to effectively observe his surroundings and memorize his gang literature when he was a teenager. They'd gone from rags to riches together, from flipping an ounce or two of cocaine every month to flipping kilos of cocaine, heroin, and fentanyl every week. From bullet wars with primitive revolvers to jumping out with 5th generation Glocks and mini-Dracos equipped with high-capacity magazines and laser sightings. From fucking hood rats in trap houses to fucking bad young bitches like Lacey and Nya in extravagant mansions with bedrooms that looked like something out of *Dupont Registry* or *Forbes* magazine. Marcus had lost other fellow gang members, but none of their deaths had hit him like Grizzy's did.

But the show had to go on, so Marcus was back on the streets. He was from 72nd and Green, but his gang and the GDs on 71st and Rhodes had a longstanding alliance. The young man who held the rank of Assistant Regent for the GDs on Rhodes was Khalil "Tito" Earl, a millionaire street nigga who was cousins with Bankroll Reese, one of the richest young niggas in Chicago. Grizzy had met Tito through his plug early last year, and the two sets of Gangster Disciples had essentially become one.

The breathtaking feeling of the head of his dick striking the back of Lacey's throat jolted Marcus out of his reverie. She dragged her soft lips to the glans and then throated him again, wrestling his Calvin Klein boxer-briefs and black Givenchy shorts farther down his thickly muscled thighs, so she could massage his balls while she fellated him.

Marcus took a swig from his gooey cup of Lean and swept his gaze across the alleyway. There were GDs everywhere. Tito's mother, Dee-Dee, the sole owner of an elite catering service, had three grills going at once, barbecuing a smorgasbord of meats and vegetables in the backyard of a property her daughter, Tinky, owned. It was a celebration of life for Grizzy, but the gang was on high alert. Though only a few of them had participated in the Highland Park shooting, every single one was responsible for the retaliatory strike on the Black P. Stones who'd placed the five-million-dollar bounty on Grizzy's head. The general of that particular faction of Black P. Stones was Johnny Broward, and Johnny's sister was Johnna Broward, the billionaire CEO of Panteon Technologies. According to Johnna's friend, Cherrelle, Johnna had given her big brother $100 million when he was released from federal prison less than two weeks ago.

And $100 million was one hell of a war chest.

Marcus' toes curled over in his Prada sneakers, and the knuckles popped as his semen spurted out into Lacey's mouth.

"Ooouuu, shit," he groaned. "Don't get none of that nut on my seat."

He said it even though he knew that the chance of Lacey allowing a single drop of semen to spill down his dick was slim to none. She was a cum-swallowing nymphomaniac. Just last night, she'd sucked three cum shots out of him, and she drank it all down like a triple shot of tequila. She did the same thing now, holding only the head of his long, black organ in her mouth and drinking from it as if it was a straw she'd skewered through the lid of a protein shake.

She sat up straight in her seat afterward, adjusting her hair in the visor mirror and reapplying a coat of iKiss lip gloss to her sexy lips. Her phone was buzzing in her oversized Gucci shoulder bag. She checked it and said, "Shit, I gotta go. Brielle said we need to get back to the mansion. Nya's having a breakdown."

"She thinks I had a hand in Grizzy gettin' killed," Marcus said. He had pulled up his shorts and underwear and taken his mini-Draco out of the door panel to lay it across his lap, and his studious eye was fixed on an AR-style pistol his close friend, Smoke, was holding as he and three more GDs stood next to the one-car garage behind Tinky's rental property.

"She does," Lacey concurred. "She actually told me that. Don't tell her I told *you* that, but she did say it. She's caught up on the fact that they knew he was in the backseat. There were only three people who knew that other than him, I mean. I don't think she's a hundred percent sure you did it, but you're the leading suspect because I was riding in that Cullinan with her, so she knows it wasn't me. And of course it wasn't her."

Marcus' lower lip slowly moved up and over his upper lip. Nya's suspicions of him weren't all that different from his suspicions of her. He'd been trying to figure out how the shooters had figured out that Grizzy was in the back of that Rolls Royce when they shot him dead. The bullets hadn't so much as grazed Marcus as he steered the six-figure exotic vehicle, and for seven or eight hours, he'd contemplated the unnerving possibility that his cousin, Grizzy's wife had ultimately orchestrated his murder. Who else could have known to shoot into the back door? Nya didn't necessarily need any part of the $5 million Bang Boy had put on Grizzy's head because, with Grizzy dead, the $20 million she and Grizzy had in their joint account became hers.

And Marcus knew a lot of women who would double-cross their husband for $20 million.

"Ain't enough money in the world for me to turn on my blood," Marcus said stiffly.

"I know that, but you can't knock her for thinking it. She's looking at Bam as a possibility too." Lacey pushed open her door. "I'll call you when I make it to the mansion. I know y'all got a lot going on over here, but your ass better be in bed with me tonight."

"I'll be there," Marcus lied as he watched Lacey climb out of his SUV and swing the door shut behind her. In truth, he'd already made plans with Ashley Daniels, the mother of three of his children. They were taking the kids to her mother in Bellwood, and then, they were flying first class to New York City to see Drake and 21 Savage in concert. Marcus had kept $450,000 out of the half million Nya paid for the hit on Bang Boy and his gang. He'd split the remaining fifty grand between the other five shooters, and he was going to give Ashley thirty grand for the household.

Marcus raised his iPhone and checked the MTN News app for the eleventh time this hour. There was an update on the Highland Park shooting. He pressed play on the news clip and watched MTN News anchor Alexandria Fisher break the news.

"The FBI has officially joined the manhunt for the six masked gunmen who were seen on a Panteon doorbell camera blocking off two Mercedes Sprinter vans in Highland Park and opening fire on its occupants, wounding all ten passengers and killing six of them, including three California residents. The Chicago Police Department released a small portion of the video to the public in hopes of identifying the shooters. Due to its graphic nature, we're only able to show the first four seconds of the video..."

The doorbell camera footage began just as Bronco —a GD he'd grown up with on 72 and Green — veered over and stopped in front of the lead Sprinter van. Marcus was half a second behind Bronco's white Buick SUV, swerving to a screeching halt in his own slime green Dodge Charger Hellcat. He and Smoke had bailed out of the Charger holding mini-Dracos with seventy shot drums and ran right at the

Sprinters with their guns raised and aimed at the driver of the lead van, who Marcus had recognized as a "White Moe" Black P. Stone named Butter.

The footage ended there, but in Marcus' mind, it continued. He could see himself squeezing the trigger. Butter's eyes had gone wide as a 7.6 millimeter round carved a fleshy hole in the front of his throat. Three or four more bullets pierced his upper chest before a rapid-fire barrage of 45-caliber rounds from Bronco's Glock pistol hit him in the face, causing his head to bounce and jerk around like a bobblehead on fast forward and spray the contents of his skull all over the headrest.

Smoke and his younger brother, Spazz, had gone for X-Man, the driver of the second Sprinter van, and once they neutralized him, the six of them — Marcus, Smoke, Spazz, Bronco, and two younger GDs named Splash and Ruger Ron — had emptied their guns into both of the Sprinters. The shooting was over twenty seconds after it began. Marcus and Bronco had covered the license plates on their vehicles shortly before the hit, and they hadn't removed the black plastic coverings until they were away from the shooting scene. The Buick Encore was set ablaze and left burning in a south side alleyway, and Marcus' Charger Hellcat was with Ruger Ron in Hammond, Indiana where it would stay until Marcus had the rims and paint changed.

Only Lacey knew that Marcus had kept the lion's share of the money Nya paid for the brazen attack on the White Moes. Marcus felt money was owed to him. He'd gone from rags to riches with Grizzy, and he was still agitated by the fact that Grizzy hadn't given him at least a couple million out of the money Grizzy and Nya had gotten from Johnna Broward. Marcus now had a little under two million dollars to his name while Nya had *ten times* that amount, not to mention a record deal that would undoubtedly bring her millions more. And the thing that was *really* grating on Marcus' nerves was the teeth clenching fact that he'd been at Grizzy's side all his life, and Grizzy hadn't even been with Nya two months before he put a ring on her finger and gave her access to all his money.

"Tender-dick niggas," Marcus muttered through clenched teeth. He shook his head and watched as Lacey and Brielle jetted off down the alley in their two black Bentley SUVs.

He started his own engine and raised his smartphone to check Bang Boy's social media pages, and as he scanned through them, searching for any signs that Bang Boy had survived the shooting, he thought of the black Audi SUV that had reversed away as he sprayed the lead Sprinter van. He'd seen a brown-skinned woman in the driver's seat, and her braided head turned to look out the rear window as she darted backwards up the street. Marcus thought he'd glimpsed someone else in the backseat, but he hadn't given it a second glance. His cousin, Alaina, had told him that Bang Boy would be seated in back of one of the Sprinters, so he and his fellow gang members had sent over two hundred rounds into the passengers' compartments of both vans. That was all that mattered.

Marcus looked up from his phone when Smoke came walking up to his door. He lowered his window a few inches, sipped from his tall cup of Lean, and grimaced as he swallowed it down.

"Folks," Smoke said, sticking his Draco down in the front of his Amiri jeans and tugging the hem of his snug-fitting, black, Amiri shirt down over the gun handle, "I just hung up from talkin' with Pandy. You know that's one of Johnna's best friends. She said Bang Boy ain't even get hit up. He was in that black Audi truck. The nigga just left the University of Chicago Medical Center, checkin' on his people. Butter, X-Man, and some lil nigga named Quan got whacked. The other three bodies was some hoes."

"I was just thinkin' about that goddamn Audi truck," Marcus spat.

"Folks n'em just saw a brown-skinned lil bitch ridin' down Green in a black Audi truck. They say she rode right past your grandma's house."

An invisible boa constrictor coiled around Marcus' lungs and squeezed all the breath out of him. Eyes wide, he stared at Smoke, a dark brown-hued street nigga with a diamond flooded Audemars Piguet watch on his wrist and fat dreadlocks hanging down around his head. He looked like Florida rapper Hotboii.

Not that Marcus was thinking about Smoke's appearance. His mind was on that black Audi truck. Bang Boy knew exactly where Ms. White lived. He'd spent plenty of afternoons there as a teenager. Grizzy's father had brought Bang Boy to the block dozens of times in the early 2000s, back when Bang Boy was Willie White's personal security, and if there was one thing Marcus knew about Johnny "Bang Boy" Broward, it was that beefing with him when he knew where to find you was not a wise move.

"Why you lookin' at me like that?" Smoke asked as he adjusted the three diamond tennis chains he wore around his neck.

"Jump in," Marcus said. "Have folks n'em follow us in one of them Hellcats. We gon' post up on Green."

"You think that was him in that Audi?"

"I know it was him."

"Aw, we on that." Smoke upped his mini-Draco with one hand and used the other to motion for the two younger gangsters who'd stood next to the garage with him. Seconds later, he was seated next to Marcus, pulling a black cotton ski mask down over his dreads but keeping the eye and mouth holes rolled up to his forehead, while Splash and Fat Folks trailed them out of the alleyway in a blacked-out Dodge Challenger Hellcat.

Chapter 16

"Hey, Mama! I miss you! I love you!"

Nya smiled and giggled at her four-year-old son, Quendell Hardiman's elated expression as his wide, brown eyes stared back at her through the screen of her iPhone. She thumbed the tears from her eyes before they could spill down her gorgeous, brown visage.

"Mama loves you too," she said, unable to repress her ear-to-ear smile. Quendell had her round, beautiful face, though his complexion was a shade or three lighter than his father, Quentis Hardiman, and a shade darker than his mother. He was talking to her on FaceTime from his bedroom in the modest two-bedroom apartment her parents had moved into while they searched for a permanent home address in Arizona.

"Grandma took me to a *big* house today," he said, extending one slender brown arm far out to his side. "It got a swimmin' pool! It got a slide that goes into the swimmin' pool! Like that water park!"

Nya burst into a fit of giggles for the second time since her son first answered the video call. She was seated on the white, leather, upholstered bench seat in her enormous walk-in closet. All of her girls were standing behind the bench, leaning in over her shoulders to wave and say hey to the handsome little devil on her smartphone screen. There was a neat mountain of bank-new hundred-dollar bills piled up to the right of her — two million dollars' worth. Resting atop the cash was her hand and three positive pregnancy tests.

"I've got a surprise for you," Nya said to Q. "A big surprise."

"Is it Disneyland?" Q's eyebrows went up in anticipation.

"It's better than Disneyland."

"Better than Sonic the Hedgehog?!"

"*Way* better."

Q's intelligent, brown eyes lit up, and he took off running, shouting for his grandma as he went.

Nya wiped more moisture from her eyelids and grinned at the bouncing view of the ceiling in her parents' apartment. Q's pattering footfalls carried him out of his bedroom and down a narrow hallway to the living room. "Grandma! My mama got a surprise way better than Disneyland! It's big!"

"Gimme this phone and stop all that doggone yellin!" Christine said, snatching the iPhone from her grandson. The shaky image became still as Christine brought the camera up to her comely brown face. "Nya, why you got this boy all worked up, and it's damn near ten o'clock at night? It's past his bedtime."

Nya snickered. Behind her, Brielle was whispering about Lacey's latest exploits —— apparently, Lacey had just sucked her boyfriend, Marcus' dick in his Benz truck, only to pull up on some ruggedly handsome, young sneaky link at a downtown hotel suite half an hour later, which explained her absence now — but Nya's mother had her full attention.

Christine Rice was thirty-seven, but she looked just as young as her daughter. They shared the same reddish-brown complexion, and both of them had sexy, round faces and charming, light brown eyes. But that was where their similarities came to an end. Christine was five-foot-one, three inches taller than her daughter. She had wider hips, thicker thighs, and a fat, round ass while Nya was more on the petite side. Christine didn't take shit from anybody, but her approach was more passive aggressive while Nya's was more... deadly.

"We looked at a few more houses today," Christine said. "Of course, Q liked the most expensive one the realtor showed us. They wanted three point four million for that damn house. I knew we couldn't afford it when we pulled up to the gate. I guess the realtor figured since our daughter's a big rap star now, we could afford to live like Cardi B."

"Tell them we want it."

Christine wrinkled her brow. She'd been bringing a Newport cigarette to her pretty, pink lips, and that hand froze in place. She was wearing an engagement ring Goldie had given her sixteen years ago when Nya was still their sweet, little girl. Nya had always asked her mother why she'd kept the ring, especially after Goldie moved on to marry and have two sons by another woman. "He'll be back," Christine would always say, and as it turned out, she was right. They'd reconnected at Nya and Grizzy's engagement party, and they'd been inseparable ever since.

"No, Nya," Christine said after a time. "I know you got a nice little signing bonus for that music, but I'm not about to have you paying a ridiculous down payment and an even crazier mortgage for a house that's way out of your budget. And besides, I'd have to find a bank that would approve that kind of loan."

"Not a loan, Mama." Nya turned the camera, so Christine could see the mountain of hundred-dollar bills piled next to her. "Cash. I got a little under $20 million in the bank and another $8 million in cash. Go ahead and tell the realtor you want that house, and I'll wire the..."

"Wait," Christine interjected, "were those pregnancy tests?" Nya cracked a hesitant smirk.

"Are you pregnant? Is that the surprise you had for Q?"

"I missed my period," Nya said with a small nod of her head. "Didn't realize it until about a week and a half ago, and

I didn't take the tests until a few minutes ago. All three showed positive results."

"You don't sound all that excited."

Nya paused to think out her response before giving voice to it. "To be honest," she said finally, "I was thinking about getting an abortion when I first figured out that I might be pregnant, but that was before Grizzy got... well, you know."

A long, gut-wrenching silence ensued. A dagger of dejection stabbed through Nya's aching heart, and she found herself thumbing tears from her eyes yet again. She sniffled. Noesha appeared with a neatly folded Kleenex tissue and pressed it against Nya's lower eyelids.

"How are you holding up now?" Christine asked.

Nya only shrugged her shoulders. "Been recording all day, tryna block it all out."

"Well," Christine reasoned, "at least his boys are out there gettin' some payback. They say all those shootings that went down earlier today had something to do with Grizzy gettin' killed last night."

"Yeah," Nya said with another sniffle. "I heard that too."

"Be safe out there, Nya. I don't know where you got all that money from, and to tell the truth, I don't wanna know. Abortion or no abortion, I'm here for you, no matter what. I'll raise the next baby just like I raised this one."

"I'm safe, Ma." Nya flicked a glance at her diamond wristwatch. It was half past nine. Sundown. Blake and the other MBM recording artists had left out about forty minutes ago. They had a sold-out show at the United Center. Nya could have gone with them to open the show with her new hit single, but she'd opted to stay home.

She told Mama and Q she loved them and would call them back in the morning. She sent $3.4 million to Christine's bank account and then pocketed her phone. Everyone but Noesha had gone out to the bedroom to give Nya privacy with Christine. Noesha was about seven feet ahead of Nya, silently admiring the brand-new Gucci handbags and heels Brielle had purchased for Nya earlier in the day.

"You can have one of those purses if you want one," Nya said as she walked up behind her friend.

Noesha shook her head no. "I blew forty bands on designer shit today. I ain't tryna be greedy." She spun around and planted her uniquely manicured hands on her Coke-bottle hips, her warm, green eyes replete with concern, her pretty, round face tilted a little to one side. "How are you feeling right now? I mean, obviously you're going through the motions, but I wanna hear it from you. What's going on in your head? What are you thinking right at this moment?"

Nya inhaled deeply, and a whistling sigh blew from between her lips. She folded her arms across her chest and really considered the questions. The only thing that came to mind was revenge. Retaliation.

"That bitch ass nigga, Bang Boy, got my husband killed," she said, vacantly eyeing the snakeskin Gucci bag Noesha had been studying a moment ago. "I know we moved kinda fast and all, and I'm not even gon' go into the whole love at first sight thing that he and I experienced. Bottom line is, he was the only man I've ever loved with everything in me, and now he's gone because of some fuck nigga named Bang Boy. I'ma fill up a cemetery over that shit."

"If that's your goal, you're well on your way to completing it. Ten bodies in less than twenty-four hours, and we haven't even caught up with Bang Boy yet."

Nya's eyes flashed from the purse to Noesha, her brow wrinkling as Noesha's words registered in her brain.

"Wait a minute," she said. "What do you mean we haven't caught up with Bang Boy?!"

"He wasn't in either one of those Sprinter vans. You know Smoke wanna get with me. He just texted me about twenty minutes ago, saying he had just found out that Bang Boy was trailing behind those two vans in a black Audi truck, and somebody just saw that same truck on 72 and Green a few hours ago."

A firestorm of anger erupted from somewhere behind Nya's sternum and rapidly spread throughout her body. She clenched her teeth. Her phone began ringing in her pocket, and she ignored it.

"Where did y'all say Lacey was?" Nya asked.

"At the W hotel with some dreadhead nigga she just met." Noesha produced her iPhone to text Lacey, but Nya waved it off.

"Find something black you can fit," Nya said, turning to rake her eyes across her extensive designer wardrobe. "We don't need Lacey. You and Niecy can slide behind me in that Cullinan I borrowed from Blake, and Quita can ride in the Bentayga with Bad Brielle."

She crossed the room to a rack of dresses and removed a black, Tucci, bandage dress from a hanger. Draping the dress over the bench, she began to undress, ignoring the distinctive ache in her heart and the dull throb of fatigue in her bones. She'd hardly gotten any sleep last night, and it didn't look like she was going to be getting any tonight.

"You gon' ride with us in the Cullinan, right?" Noesha asked.

Nya shook her head no as she took the Glock pistol out of her panties and stuck it down in a new, black, leather, Gucci bag. "I'm riding by myself in another one of Blake's cars. Shit, I might try to buy it from him."

"What kinda car is it?" Noesha was peeling off her orange and white Chanel ensemble, glancing back at the doorway as the other girls spilled back into the walk-in closet.

"It's a black-on-black Bugatti Veyron Super Sport. Fastest production car on the planet." Nya pulled the tight-fitting dress down over her slender little body, slipped on a pair of black, leather, Bucci sneakers, shouldered her purse, and picked up her mini-Draco. "When I pull up on niggas in that Bugatti and hop out on em with this Draco, they ain't gon' be able to see what hit em."

Chapter 17

At four hundred sixty-seven feet above Carnegie Hill, Johnna Broward's thirty-million-dollar home in the sky, uniquely positioned at the highest elevation point on Manhattan's coveted Upper East Side, dominated the skyline from every angle. The five-bedroom triplex at 180 East 88th Street crowned the fifty-story building, which looked like something out of Dubai. The penthouse spanned 5,508 square feet with an additional 3,501 square feet of terraces, including a breathtaking rooftop with a bird's-eye view of Central Park. Made of glass and concrete, the apartment featured jaw-dropping arches, brass-framed windows, and white-oak flooring that was salvaged from the Admont Abbey, a Benedictine monastery in Austria.

A sweeping white sculptural spiral staircase was the pièce de résistance, and descending the staircase usually put Johnna in a particularly jovial mood.

Now, though, that was not the case.

Johnna held a ball glass in one nervous hand and her iPhone in the other. Two inches of Rare Hare "Lapine" cognac sloshed to and fro inside the glass as she walked down the steps in a fresh, pink, Versace robe. A few drops of Visine had erased the red veins from the whites of her eyes, but her eyelids were still squinted from the blunt of exotic marijuana she'd smoked in her bathtub. She'd swallowed a thirty-milligram Percocet pill to help settle her nerves, but there was no way to wash away her worries completely.

The FaceTime call she'd received from Johnny was what had her on edge.

He'd told her about the deadly Highland Park shooting, but she wasn't really concerned about that; Johnny had lost two of his very best friends, and the other two were hospitalized with multiple gunshot wounds, but Johnny was perfectly fine, and Johnna knew that he and his gang were going to push on Grizzy's set of Gangster Disciples for the retaliatory attack. The unnerving fact that Johnny had canceled his flight plans was what had Johnna self-medicating with drugs and alcohol. Johnny wasn't coming to New York, so there was no one to stop Diana Caldwell from meeting with the FBI.

"Shit," Johnna muttered. "I must have the worst luck in the world."

Tip Stingley was seated Indian style on the sofa near the base of the staircase, a Wahida Clark novel open on her lap, her head bobbing to the beat of whatever music was playing from the AirPods in her ears. She happened to be looking up from her book when Johnna appeared ten feet to the left of her, and though she didn't hear the words come out of Johnna's mouth, she did see Johnna's lips moving.

So, Tip removed one AirPod and said, "Huh?"

Johnna shook her head. She was too frustrated to repeat the pessimistic statement. "My brother's not coming," she said, dropping her surgically fattened ass onto the sofa. "I don't know what to do."

Folding her book shut and placing it on the round, glass table in front of her, Tip said, "Why ain't he coming? I mean, I know you expressed the *urgency* of this shit. We *need* him."

"It's that shooting that's all over the news right now. They were gunning for him." Johnna went to the MTN News app on her smartphone and then handed it over to her assistant. "Go ahead. Read it. They killed two of his best friends. One of their nephews. Three bitches from somewhere in California. Now, my brother's riding around looking for the gang that did it, and he's not gonna rest until he finds them."

While Tip read the news article, Johnna stared vacantly at the seven other books on her glass-top table — novels by K'wan, Zane, and Ashley and Jaquavis, Michelle Obama's latest memoir — and tried to come up with a plan to stop Diana Martin-Caldwell from talking.

Tip handed the phone back a moment later. She unfolded her meaty legs and picked up her own phone from beside her.

"I still got Diana's number," she said, watching Johnna sip from the glass of sixty-year-old cognac. "I could call the bitch. Offer her some money or something. Shit, you paid out a few hundred million to settle all those other lawsuits. It won't hurt to dish out another forty or fifty million. You could have your lawyer put a stipulation in the settlement offer that restricts her from making any statements against you and everyone else at Panteon."

Johnna grimaced as she swallowed the expensive liquor, thinking that maybe Tip was right. She didn't want to give that big, ugly bitch one red cent, but her pride wasn't worth jeopardizing her whole empire. She'd come from the wretched squalor of her mother's south side Chicago apartment to being number ninety-two on *Forbes* magazine's list of the world's wealthiest individuals, and she wasn't about to let some miserable widow trick her out of her spot.

And besides, what was $50 million to $14 billion?

Johnna began nodding her head. Smiling. Tip was nodding too, only her nod was in sync with the music she was listening to in one ear. Johnna looked over at Tip and rolled her lashy hazel eyes.

"What are you listening to?" Johnna asked, taking the other AirPod from Tip's hand and pushing it in her ear.

"This that *Just Left the Yard* by Dev Demetries. He used to go by D-Bo. The nigga got flow, and he's from Indiana like me. I fucks with them Nap Town niggas. Especially D.B., Fatty Stilkountin, and Mobfam E. They go hard."

Johnna had never heard of any of the rappers — she was a Chicago girl, and the only rappers she liked listening to were fellow Chicagoans Lil Durk, Polo G, G Herbo, and King Von — but she listened to the Dev Demetries song and found that she truly enjoyed it. So much so that she went on iTunes and purchased the rapper's *Million Dollar Scars* album.

"So," Tip asked, "what it's gon' be? You want me to call this bitch or not? She might be sleep, but I'll wake her snitchin' ass right up if that's what you want me to do."

Johnna sighed and gave Tip an affirmative nod, raking her eyes up Tip's sexy, brown legs and the gray yoga shorts that left very little to the imagination. Her nipples were prominent in the white Gucci tube top she wore, and as she surfed her way down the long list of contacts in her phone, Johnna stared wantonly at the outline of her thick-lipped vagina, wondering how pretty it would look without the shorts on.

Johnna Broward was a proud member of the LGBTQ community. To her, a fat, wet pussy was just as enticing as a fat, black dick. The inebriating combination of weed, Percocet, and cognac had an arousing effect on Johnna. It always did. She could feel her vaginal juices burgeoning, her nipples hardening, as Tip put the call to Diana on speaker and listened to the trilling ring. Johnna was a hopeless nympho, her libido so overcharged that she had a handsome Dominican boyfriend *and* a sexy Colombian girlfriend to keep her insatiable sexual appetite in check. But her lovers were of no use to her now. Her girlfriend, Evita, was in Cannes, France, capitalizing off her beauty by participating in a *Vogue* magazine photo shoot for fashion mogul Anna Wintour. Her boyfriend was in Santo Domingo, visiting his ailing grandmother.

Diana answered after four rings. "Hello?"

It was a FaceTime video call. Johnna could see Diana's flashy round face on Tip's phone screen. Looked like the big girl had shed some weight over the last month or so. Johnna studied the background and saw that Diana was standing on the front porch of a brownstone building, the porch light burning bright behind her left shoulder.

"Hey, girl," Tip said seriously. "We need to talk."

Diana's dark eyes became alert very suddenly, flitting from one side of the phone screen to the other.

"Are you with Johnna right now?" And before Tip had time to voice a reply, Diana continued on. "Listen, Johnna's the sole reason my husband is six feet underground right now. She stole $23 million from Michael's gang and had the audacity to hire him at the company she started with *their* money. So what her brother was one of the original White Moes? Bang Boy certainly had a claim to some of those millions, but so did Michael Caldwell. And if those dirty millions were laundered through Panteon Technologies and turned into *billions*, then my deceased husband deserved a portion of that money too. He had every right to run into that building with guns blazing. I'd have reacted in similar fashion."

"Then why don't you just ask her for some of the money? If you believe she really did steal it, you'd be much better off coming to her than going to the courts. You're involving people who would love nothing more than to see a wealthy, Black woman like Johnna lose everything she has."

"Well," Diana reasoned, swatting a moth from in front of her face, "she should've reached out to me before the police did."

"She's willing to settle all this out of count. We can have the paperwork drawn up and faxed to your lawyer first thing tomorrow. All you have to do is agree not to make any damaging statements against Johnna and anyone else at Panteon."

Diana went silent. She glanced at something offscreen, and when her eyes shifted back to the camera, they were narrowed to a squint.

"What made her have you reach out to me today? Of all days, why today? Hm?"

Tip lifted her shoulders and let them fall back in place. It was an innocent shrug. "No real reason," she said. "It was really my idea. I figured I'd try my hand at mediating the situation. No sense in watching two of my good friends duke it out in a count room when all this can be settled in private. Plus, you know it'll keep you from looking like the Black woman who helped bring down another Black woman."

A second spell of silence ensued. Johnna's nipples were stiff, and her pussy was throbbing, but she was business-minded enough to keep her focus on the situation at hand.

"I find it funny," Diana said, her beady eyes still a squint, "that you just so happened to contact me the night before I'm scheduled to meet with the FBI. You wouldn't have happened to hear about *that*, would you? And tell the truth."

Tip was quick on the draw. "The FBI? What?! Okay, first off, that's crazy. And secondly, how in the hell would we know that?"

Yet another tense silence. Johnna got up from the sofa and went to one of the tall windows. She gazed out at the wide concrete terrace for a brief moment and then raised her iPhone to scroll through her Instagram notifications. She'd only thumbed through a few of them when Diana spoke again.

"Okay, what's the offer?" Diana asked finally.

"Twenty-five million. It's the most she can give up without risking an inquiry from Panteon investors."

Johnna grinned and glanced back at her assistant, proud that Tip had come up with such an elaborate lie so quickly.

"That's only ten percent of what I'm suing for," said Diana.

"If you help the FBI bring down Panteon, you won't get ten cents."

Three contemplative seconds later, Diana said, "I can't say it's not a tempting offer, but to be honest with you, it's about more than the coins. Michael's dead. I wish the same fate for Johnna Broward. So whether or not I get paid, I'll be just as happy as long as she ends up in a prison cell for the next nine or ten years. And you can tell her I said that."

Johnna's teeth came together with an audible click. Her gaze was on her phone screen — some up-and-coming boxer from the Bronx named Bruce Carrington had just followed her on Instagram, and she'd gone to a video on his page that showed him sparring with his trainer — but her mind went blank as she spun around to look at Tip.

"She hung up," Tip said.

A low, guttural growl emanated from deep within Johnna's throat. She stormed off in a blind rage, muttering expletives as she rounded the sofas, the tail of her robe billowing up around her thickly toned legs. Tip was seconds behind her.

"See if you can get ahold of Alexus," Johnna said snappishly. "Let her know that this grizzly bear faced bitch has her mind set on being a rat and other ideas."

Following Johnna up the staircase, Tip tried phoning Alexus while Johnna tried to call Johnny. Neither of them got an answer. When Johnny's voicemail came on, Johnna came dangerously close to slamming her phone.

She let out another low growl. She rolled her eyes and fluttered` her lashes.

"Do you know any street niggas out here in New York?" Johnna asked Tip as they approached the top of the staircase.

"Not really. I haven't gone out since I moved here. My roommate might know some people. She's a bottle girl at Angels. I'm sure she runs across dope boys and gang members every night."

"Get her on the phone." Johnna entered her lavish bedroom, untying her bathrobe and letting it fall to the floor, revealing her silky smooth, naked body. She caught a glimpse of Tip's stunned expression but thought nothing of it as she went to her closet and picked out a risqué, black, Chanel minidress. She had a huge crush on her assistant, but her own financial well-being superseded her sexual hunger.

"What should I tell her?" Tip asked.

"I've got a half million in cash sitting in my safe," Johnna replied. "If she can get somebody to go over there and put a bullet in Diana's head, she can have every dollar of it."

Chapter 18

Diana Martin-Caldwell felt a mad rush of excitement as she rudely ended the call with Tip Stingley and brought her Salem Lights cigarette up to her mouth for a long, satisfying puff.

$25 million, she thought hotly. *That conniving bitch has fourteen billion, and she offers me $25 million?!*

The strand of thought was snipped short when a dark-colored BMW coupe came lancing up the street in her direction. She froze, thinking of the warning that a silver-haired NYPD detective had given her earlier. But her fear was unwarranted. There was a party taking place at the end of the block, and the two young, Black men in the Beamer were merely showing off for the girls who were standing out on the sidewalk. Diana chuckled when she realized what was going on, shaking her head and letting out a breath she hadn't even realized she was holding in.

Taking another hit from her cigarette, Diana checked the time on her Apple watch. Half past eleven. She was scheduled to meet with the FBI in just six and a half hours. Part of her wanted to accept the settlement offer, but she knew that was the part that pined for the so-called American Dream. Her aching heart told her otherwise. She wanted to *destroy* Johnna Broward. For all the tearful nights she'd spent scrolling through her smartphone's photo gallery, looking at pics of a smiling husband she would never see again. For all the horrible things the media had said about him in the days and weeks after the Panteon workplace shooting. Diana wanted the world to know the dark truth about the wealthy young CEO of Panteon Technologies, and there wasn't enough money in the world to dissuade her from speaking that truth.

She could not *wait* to speak with the FBI.

"See how cocky she acts when her ass is locked away in Federal prison," Diana muttered heatedly. She took one last drag on her cancer stick and extinguished it under her shoe, a conspiratorial smirk lifting one side of her mouth as she envisioned Johnna curled up on a prison bunk with tears of regret cascading down her cheeks.

Diana was turning to head back inside for the night when she spotted a familiar looking SUV rounding the corner onto Jamaica Avenue. It was the blacked-out Ford Expedition the two NYPD detectives had picked her up in, and as it slowed to a stop at the curb, she saw through the open passenger's window that the Black female detective was in the driver's seat. The man seated next to her was not Detective McKenzie. He was much younger, early or mid-thirties, and he looked like he might be Hispanic. The arm resting on the frame of the passenger's door was huge.

Diana walked hurriedly down the steps, up the short brick walkway, and across the sidewalk. The Hispanic man reached out and shook her hand as she approached his door.

"Well," Detective Sinclair said, "I'm glad we caught you standing out here on the porch. I'd have hated to knock on your door at this time of night, but I wouldn't have had much of a choice."

"What's going on?" Diana asked. Her eyes were on the Hispanic man. His plain, black tee seemed too small for all the muscles in his torso. He wore his police badge on a silver necklace. If he was a Mexican, he was the tallest Mexican Diana had ever seen. The brownest too. It was like maybe he trained with Dwayne "The Rock" Johnson.

"There's a bounty on your head," Sinclair explained in the most urgent of tones. "We intercepted a call from one of Johnna Broward's close associates. The FBI assessed it as a credible threat, and I've been instructed to bring you in now. Get in."

Diana sucked in an apprehensive breath. Her eyes went wide with fear. She wondered how the NYPD had learned of her son's home address. Then she figured that if an underfunded police department could track her down, a multimillionaire like Johnna Broward would have no trouble doing it.

So, she snatched open the Expedition's rear door and climbed in, texting her daughter-in-law as she did it. She told Cara to lock all the doors and that she'd be back soon, and when she looked up from her phone a few seconds later, the Expedition was already racing off down Jamaica Avenue.

"How did they know where to find me?" Diana asked. Then, "Shit, how did *you* know where to find me? I never gave you this address. Never gave it to Makenzie either."

"Are you familiar with Alexus Costilla?" Sinclair checked her rearview mirror. "Queen A?"

"Of course I'm familiar with Queen A. Who isn't? She's married to that fine ass Bulletface, and she's the wealthiest woman in the world. But what does she have to do with any of this?"

Sinclair offered no reply. Instead, she turned her head and gave the Hispanic cop a somewhat agitated look, and he swiveled in his seat to look back at Diana.

"Plato o plomo," he said, enunciating each word of the Spanish phrase. "Silver or lead. One of Queen A's favorite ultimatums. Had you been as smart as you thought you were, you'd have taken the silver."

The brawny Mexican man moved fast, drawing a large, black pistol with a long sound suppressor screwed into its barrel from his shoulder holster and aiming it at Diana's forehead.

She never even saw the flash.

Chapter 19

Near the corner of Cicero and Gladys on Chicago's west side, there was a food truck with *Highway Beat* emblazoned above the serving window in gold, block lettering. The two young, Black women inside the food truck were Coco and Tori Kelly, U.T.'s oldest daughters. There was a white, plastic armchair just outside the serving window where U.T. usually sat on busy nights like tonight, but now, the chair was vacant because U.T. had gotten word that Grizzy's wife had put a half a million dollars on his bald scalp, and he wasn't taking any chances.

His girlfriend, Shameika, had parked his Jeep Grand Wagoneer two car lengths behind the food truck, and now, she was in the backseat right beside him, studying the social media pages that belonged to Nya and her Plush Gang sorority.

One of the two carloads behind them was younger gang members who'd trailed them and was parked across the street. The other one was farther down the block. Every single one of the vigilant young Undertaker Vice Lords was armed, and so was U.T. He had a Kel-Tek .223 with a one hundred-round drum magazine stretched across his lap, and he was sipping from a fresh pint of Hennessy cognac, his eyes flicking from side to side as he observed the block from behind his darkly tinted windows.

"Okay, Nya finally posted something," Shameika said, handing her Samsung smartphone over to U.T. "It's for her husband."

U.T. accepted the phone and looked at the post. It was a video collage of photos and videos, some showing Grizzy standing alone, others showing him with Nya. She'd captioned it with two emojis, a brown pair of prayer hands and a red broken heart. She'd selected a rap song for the Instagram video collage, and it was the song's lyrics that got U.T.'s attention.

The song was *Get Buck* by Mo3, and it was clearly a message to whoever was responsible for Grizzy's murder.

"Did that for my dawg, yeah this that get back
When it's war, yeah, we go tit for tat
Ring around the rosie with this big Mac
Don't come around if we don't know you,
Getcho shit clapped..."

U.T. watched the video collage twice more before handing the phone back to Shameika. He sat thinking after that. Fuming really. Puncho had gone behind his back and figured out that Bang Boy had actually put *five* million dollars on Grizzy's head, and he knew that Puncho had sent Bang Boy the video showing that it was him and his nephew, Lil Pistol, who'd committed the murder. U.T. had called Puncho's phone eight or nine times, and he'd sent half a dozen text messages. Puncho had yet to answer his phone. The texts showed that he'd seen them, but he had yet to reply to any of them.

"He's a real fuck nigga for getting you into this shit and then not bothering to answer his goddamn phone," Shameika said, reading U.T.'s mind. "I say you should get on his people over this shit, but the nigga ain't really got no people. His mama died of cancer, and you know he lost his sister to Covid. Now that his nephew's dead, it's just him, his niece, his son. He probably already got them outta town. Especially if he got that money from Bang Boy!"

U.T. nodded his fat, bald head. He took another face-twisting swig from his cognac. In his peripheral, he watched a dark-colored Buick sedan pull over across the street from him. Two sexy, young, Black girls got out and crossed the street to the food truck, joining a line of eight other Black Chicagoans.

"Puncho done fucked up this time," he said after a moment. "That lil bitch, Nya, did too. I don't give a fuck what she did in these streets. My lil niggas wit' all that. I don't know who hyped that bitch up, got her to thinkin' she can put money on my head, but it's about to backfire on her stupid ass. I can guarantee you that. See, I gave her a pass when they said she was the one who got my cousin, Sleet, killed, but that was because she a little ass girl, and her pops, Goldie, was my nigga back in the day. I ain't givin' out no more passes. It's her ass this time."

"They say Goldie moved to Arizona a few weeks ago." Shameika was on Puncho's Instagram page now, lurking, even though he hadn't posted anything in two days. "You know, it's sad too because I was just starting to like Young Nya's music. The bitch went hard on the song she got with Bulletface. Now she a whole opp. That shit wild."

U.T. picked up his own smartphone and tried calling Puncho again. When the voicemail came on, he slammed a fingertip down on the *End Call* button and turned back to his window. Scowling. Gritting his teeth. He saw that OTF rapper Doodie Lo had just pulled up in a blue and gray Dodge Challenger Hellcat on Forgiato rims and hopped out with three more gang members. Highway Beef was a popular food truck, and there were celebrity sightings all the time, but several girls reacted as if Doodie was the first celeb they'd ever seen, rushing over to him with their phones in hand, recording video of themselves hugging him for their social media pages. U.T. was observing all the commotion with a stone face when his phone rang with a callback from Puncho. He answered quickly.

It was a video call. Puncho was sitting down. He wore a Dior bucket hat over a matching shirt. A diamond necklace. He had a thick blunt wedged behind one ear, and his dreads were braided into five long ropes. The whites of his eyes were dark red, and there was a big-bootied woman lying naked in bed behind him; U.T. could see her in the reflection of a mirror over Puncho's shoulder, a brown skinned girl with an enormous ass that clearly had several wet ribbons of semen splashed across its smooth slopes.

"What's up?" Puncho asked drably.

U.T. snapped. "What the fuck you mean what's up? What the fuck you *think* up? Nigga, you went behind my back and pulled that bitch ass move, and now, *I* gotta deal with the shit. Now some bitch done put a half ticket on my head over some bullshit I ain't have nothin' to do with."

"You lied to me, big homie. You told me dude had a million on Grizzy's head. Come to find out, he had five Ms on that nigga. You tried to play me, so I played you. That's the way the game goes. Should've played it fair."

"You know ain't no comin' back to the hood, right? It's up there, lil nigga. I bet not catch you out west."

Puncho scoffed at the threat. He was incredibly unattractive, the kind of guy who'd never fucked a bad bitch in his life, but the designer hat and shirt and the diamonds glistening around his neck gave him a certain level of appeal. He had money now. Even Shameika was looking at him with a newfound attraction, leaning in close to U.T. and staring down at Puncho with a huge smile on her dark brown face.

"You're forgetting something," Puncho said, and suddenly, his full lips spread into a shit-eating grin. "I just got five Ms. The whole purpose of that mission was to get the fuck *outta* the hood. You think I wanna stay in that raggedy mothafucka? And secondly, if and when I ever feel like coming back, I'll do just that. And do you know why?"

U.T. only stared at his former protege. His adrenal glands were on fire. His foot was shaking on the floorboard. He wanted to reach through the phone with the barrel of his rifle and blow that godawful grin off Puncho's ugly fucking face. "I got bread now, nigga," Puncho said. "*Millions!* You paid Tyrin three bands to whack that last nigga. Just imagine how fast he'll move when I offer him *thirty* bands. Think, nigga. Use your fuckin' brain. You don't wanna threaten somebody who just got paid five Ms to step on a nigga. Especially not when that somebody knows your every move." He raised an impressive pile of cash, six or seven ten-thousand-dollar packets of bank new hundreds, all of them rubber-banded together. "See this? Seventy bands. This *way* more than enough to get the job done. *Think.*"

Clenching his teeth, U.T. glanced up at a passing SUV that had garnered a lot of attention as it rounded the corner onto Gladys. It was a black Bentley Bentayga. Most likely another celebrity. Yo Gotti had pulled through in a fleet of white Rolls Royces just last week. Had U.T. not been so upset, he'd have watched the Bentayga as it pulled to a stop in the middle of the street, two car lengths ahead of the food truck. But he *was* upset. *Highly* upset.

"You taught me everything I know." Puncho went on as he took the blunt from behind his ear, stuck it between his fat lips, and put fire to the end of it. "You can think real good when that liquor ain't in you. Put down that bottle. I know you got it right there with you. If I was on bullshit, I would've paid somebody to spin through there and air out you and that food truck. That's probably where you at right now, ain't it?"

There was no reply from U.T. He sat there, thinking, trying to concentrate. His ears were ringing, and he realized his blood pressure was up. He hadn't taken his Amlodipine this afternoon. The one thought that emerged through the fog of his alcohol-clouded brain was the hard fact that Puncho knew exactly where to hit him. His daughters were his Achilles heel. Not many people outside of his immediate circle were familiar with his family, but Puncho knew Tori and Coco personally. He'd gone to Fenger High School with Coco, and he'd been known to be overprotective of both sisters as if they were his own siblings. U.T. had to be mindful of that vulnerability.

"So," he asked, forcing himself to speak in a calmer tone of voice, "you really got the whole five million out that nigga, huh?"

Puncho nodded. "Gave the bitch who set the pick a million for putting in that work for me, but the other four mine. And for the record, I'm the one who told Kiesha to let Tyrin know about the half a ticket Nya put on your head. You should be thanking me."

"Thanks," U.T. said, not meaning it at all.

"You should be good for now. Word ain't spread yet about that bag shorty put on you. I would stay out the streets for the next few weeks though. Just to be on the safe side."

The ember at the end of Puncho's overstuffed blunt glowed red as he toked on it. The girl lying on the bed behind him started to get up, rising onto all fours, and U.T. caught a captivating glimpse of her glistening wet pussy. The glutinous ropes of cum on her bountiful butt cheeks sluiced down to the backs of her meaty thighs as she moved across the bed on her knees, and then, she was gone from the background, leaving U.T. with a growing erection that was likely much too short to slide in between all the ass she possessed.

"I'm sorry to hear about Lil Pistol," U.T. lied. "You know that was my lil nigga."

"That lil rap bitch killed him. Hit him with a Draco. I watched her do it." There was a rush of emotion in Puncho's tone as he muttered the words. His red-veined eyes grew watery. He sniffled and inhaled a plume of smoke and nodded his big, ugly head. "It's cool though. You know how I move. I'ma get my lick back eventually. My niece, Teyana, ain't stopped cryin' over her brother yet, but shit, I just gave her a hundred thousand and told her to get out of town until the funeral. I'm about to do the same shit. Fuck Chicago. It's time to go."

"Stay safe, lil nigga." U.T. teared up, and he hated himself for doing it. He was pissed at Puncho, but he couldn't quell the emotions that came from raising the hideous creature from a ruthless young teen to an even more dangerous thirty-year-old man. He rested the pint-sized bottle of cognac against his vastly sloping gut and brought his thumb and forefinger together over his eyes to wipe away the moisture. "Just hit me up when you get situated. And don't think I'm over what you did either. You still got some explaining to do."

Puncho chuckled once and ended the call, and U.T. looked up from his phone just as the doors of the Bentayga swung open. Two brown-skinned girls with flawless figures stepped out and smiled for the eight or nine smartphone cameras that turned their way. There was a song playing loudly from the Bentley's sound system, and the two girls garnered even more attention as they grabbed their knees and made their fat, round asses bounce to the beat.

Judging from the way everyone seemed to converge on the twerking duo, the two girls were quite popular. U.T. buzzed his window down an inch and listened to the cacophony of voices as just about everyone on the block directed their attention at the two girls.

Someone said, "That's Quita, ain't it?"

Someone else shouted, "Uh-oh! Plush Gang in this bitch!"

Knitting his brow, U.T. tried remembering where he'd heard that name. He was still thinking it over when the front passenger's door was suddenly snatched open, and by the time he turned to see who it was, the small woman was already in the seat.

It was Nya Mixon.

Her head was mostly hidden inside the hood of a black hooded sweatshirt, but it was definitely her; U.T. had been studying her social media photos for the past few hours. She held twin Glocks with thirty-shot clips sticking out from under her small, pretty hands, aiming one at U.T.'s face and the other at Shameika.

"Go ahead and push that gun down to the floor," she said coldly. "One wrong move and I'll splash your brains all over that headrest."

Chapter 20

Nya could feel her heart pounding in her chest as the fat man's assault rifle thumped to the floorboard. Quita and Brielle had succeeded in taking everyone's attention off the boss of the Undertaker Vice Lords, but there was no telling how long it would be before his goons noticed that he'd been taken hostage.

"You," Nya said to the girl. "Get up here and pull off. If you scream or do anything stupid, I'm killing you *and* him. And these Glocks got switches on em. I'll let off this whole sixty before your guys can even reach me."

The girl moved shakily but quickly. Within thirty seconds, she had climbed in between the front seats and started the engine. Nya ordered her to make a U-turn and drive off down Cicero Avenue. Noesha fell in line behind them in the Bugatti, followed closely by Niecy in the Cullinan, and when the fat man's phone rang on his lap, Nya glowered at him.

"I know that's your boys," she said. "Tell him you'll be right back. Say anything else and I'll have my niggas put a hundred holes in that food truck. I got two shooters in the backseat of that Bentayga with their guns aimed at Tori and Coco right now as we speak. Play if you want to."

Nya stared him down as he answered the call and followed her directions. She was glad he hadn't called her bluff. There was no one in the backseat of Brielle's Bentley truck. She had learned that U.T.'s daughters worked the famous Highway Beef food truck from Niecy, who'd briefly dated an Undertaker named Tyrin two summers ago. Niecy had offered Tyrin $50,000 cash for everything he knew about Dwayne Kelly, better known as U.T., and Tyrin had taken the bait. He'd described U.T.'s vehicles and told her where to find U.T. and his daughters. That was all the information Nya needed.

She had an AirPod in one ear. The three-way call she'd made to Niecy and Noesha was still running. Brielle and Quita were also on the line, though the two of them had muted their end to keep the Megan Thee Stallion song they were twerking to from interfering with the call.

The girl behind the wheel — Tyrin had told Niecy that her name was Shameika — started crying. "I just lost my baby in a house fire a few weeks ago," she sobbed. "I don't want anything to do with this shit. I don't do this street shit. I'm a registered nurse. I'm not even connected to U.T. like that. I got a husband at home. This just my side nigga."

"Shut the fuck up," Nya said, emphasizing each word. She flicked her fiery gaze back over to U.T. "Hey, fat boy. I already know you sent your guys to kill my husband. Tell me who the other shooter was and maybe I'll spare you. *Maybe*."

He stared back at her, picked up the pint of Hennessy that was leaning against his huge belly, and drank from it. "You's a bold bitch, you know that? I mean *bold*. I done heard all about you. You and Grizzy. Y'all killed my cousin, Sleet, and half of his gang. You whacked a couple of the Wicked Town TVLs. You even..."

"Who was the other shooter?" Nya cut in.

When U.T. didn't answer fast enough, Shameika said, "It was Puncho. His nephew, Lil Pistol, got killed in the shooting, and Puncho got a graze wound. Somebody paid him $5 million to do it."

"Where can I find him?" Nya asked, and before U.T. or Shameika could answer the question, Niecy spoke through the speaker in Nya's ear! "Puncho stays over there on Keelen, right down the street from Cocky Lord."

Shameika said, "He's leaving the city. U.T. literally just hung up from talking to him. And he didn't tell us where he was going."

U.T. sat forward and punched the back of the driver's seat, and Nya saw the conflagration of fury burn its way across Shameika's face as she whipped over into an alleyway and stomped down on the pedal. She spun around in her seat and scowled at the older man.

"Nigga, you ain't about to get me killed out here!" Shameika exclaimed. "The fuck you think this is?! Shit, fuck you *and* Puncho! You ain't got shit but four inches for a bitch anyway. If not for yo' tongue and that lil bit of money you got, you wouldn't be worth jack shit."

Nya fought off the overwhelming urge to laugh as she raked her eyes around the shadowy alleyway. Noesha and Niecy had just swerved into the alley behind the Jeep Grand Wagoneer, their headlights illuminating the way, but there were still some dark corners. A gauntly built older man in a stained and wrinkled white shirt stood leaning against the side of a rust-laden, brown, Chevy van, nodding off opioids. An equally emaciated prostitute wearing hardly anything sauntered out from beside a garage, fixing her black, leather miniskirt. Farther down the alley, a phalanx of gangbangers lingered outside the large, open door of another garage, and Nya figured a dice game was likely underway.

She resettled her gaze on U.T. as Niecy and Noesha rushed out of their vehicles wearing pink ski masks over their faces, Niecy toting Nya's Draco, Noesha holding her own Glock pistol with an attached fifty-round drum magazine.

"He's in the backseat," Nya said, and a second later, Noesha opened U.T's door and balled the collar of his red Scaled Fresh Apparel tee in one fist.

131

"Get the fuck out the truck," Noesha barked, pressing the barrel of her pistol against U.T.'s jaw.

Nya took the key out of the Jeep's ignition as she watched the fat man struggle to pull himself out of the open door with Noesha yanking him by the collar. Opening her own door, Nya glanced back at Shameika. "Don't try nothin'," she warned.

Shameika raised her trembling hands in surrender, the frightened look in her eyes showing that she wasn't about to try anything.

Just then, Nya heard a devastating smack of flesh colliding with flesh, followed by the thud of a body hitting the ground, and the next thing she knew, U.T. was sprinting off down the gangway next to the house they had stopped behind, his chubby, little legs propelling him down the concrete walkway much faster than Nya had thought possible.

She ran around the front of the Jeep and sent a volley of gunfire down the gangway, but U.T. ducked low and disappeared through a hole in the chain link fence.

"That bitch ass nigga!" Niecy shouted.

Nya glanced at the unconscious body lying just outside the Jeep's open rear door. It was Noesha, lying supine with her glazed-over green eyes peering vacantly at the star-sequined sky above. Niecy was squatting beside her, looking worried.

Awakened by the abrupt burst of gunfire, the nodding drug addict came to life and struck off running, while the prostitute and her trick both lowered their heads and dipped low around the side of the Chevy van. The boys standing outside the garage a few houses down the alleyway ducked for cover and drew pistols from under their shirts.

"Ay, y'all, get that bitch in the alley!" U.I. shouted from somewhere nearby. "She the one killed Pistol!"

Nya immediately recognized the change in the demeanors of some of the boys up the alley. They went from ducking for cover to standing upright, from holding their guns down at their sides to raising and aiming them in Nya's direction.

"Shit," she said and opened fire on the crowd of gang members, knowing that they were Undertaker Vice Lords just like U.T. She fired with both pistols, holding them out in front of her and sending a hail of fully automatic gunfire at the boys before they could get off a single shot.

In her peripheral, she saw Niecy appear beside her, struggling to control the mini-Draco as she fired it with reckless abandon. Five of the boys fell wounded to the ground within the first two seconds of gunfire, which was all it took Nya to empty the remainder of her sixty rounds. Three others limped quickly to one side of the alley and vanished from sight.

Nya was ejecting the depleted clips from her pistols and reaching for the extra thirty-shot clips she had in the front pocket of her hoodie when, out of the corner of her eye, she glimpsed three quick flashes of gunfire. Instinctively, she crouched low and turned that way — in the direction U.T. had escaped.

Which was when she saw him in the gangway, just his head, shoulder, and one arm, reaching through the chain-link fence and aiming a gun at her and Niecy.

Shooting.

With a panic-stricken gasp, Nya dived toward Niecy — who had stopped firing the Draco but was still holding it on the boys down the alley — and tackled her to the ground, wincing fearfully as bullets kicked dirt and rocks near her head. Her ears rang from all the stentorian booms, and her adrenaline was on full rush mode, but she managed to twist onto her back and load another thirty-round clip into one of her pistols. She hurriedly jacked the slide and sent a barrage of 40-caliber ammunition up the gangway, watching bullets stitch holes alongside the garage all the way to U.T., who fell away with an audible groan.

She was back on her feet in an instant, stuffing the Glocks in her hoodie pocket and taking possession of the Draco as Niecy dragged Noesha through what seemed like a pool of spent shell casings to the Rolls Royce Cullinan.

Nya walked backwards toward the blacked-out Bugatti Veyron, holding the Draco on the boys three garages down and squinting against the haze of gun smoke. A few of them were writhing in agony; a few others weren't moving at all. When one of them popped out from beside a newer model Cadillac sedan and let off a couple of shots at her, she shot back, even as the sting of a bullet piercing the flesh of her left thigh made her clench her teeth.

Before she knew it, she was standing next to the Bugatti's open driver door. Glancing back over her shoulder, she saw that Noesha was starting to regain consciousness, making it easier for Niecy to help her onto the backseat of the Cullinan. Nya crouched low behind the door and fired over the top of it while Niecy got her sister situated, and when Niecy got in behind the wheel of the Cullinan and peeled off in reverse, Nya slipped into the Bugatti and did the same thing, tossing the Draco onto the passenger seat as she veered wildly onto Cicero Avenue and threw the car in drive.

She checked the rearview mirror and saw police lights two blocks back. Stepping down on the gas pedal, she held on tightly to the steering wheel as the powerful engine shot her forward down the street, and when she looked in the rearview mirror a few seconds later, she was eight blocks ahead of the cop car, swerving onto a highway off ramp and racing off down the Eisenhower Expressway.

Chapter 21

The naked girl must have had a particularly ugly face because the gang had put a brown paper bag over her head and cut a hole where her mouth was, and now, two of them were fucking her on an air mattress in the living room of a trap house on 72nd and Green.

Seven members of the Gangster Disciples had fucked her already. Marcus wasn't one of them. He stood silently in the doorway, sipping Lean from his Styrofoam cup and staring emptily at the big-bootied yellow bone as she took dick in her mouth and asshole like a veteran porn actress.

Marcus' mind was somewhere else. It was nearing midnight, and his gang had yet to see that black Audi truck again. He had ten teenaged gang members posted up on the block — ducked off in gangways and laid back inside several vehicles and nine more watching from the windows of three different houses. All of them were on the lookout for that Audi, but none of them had seen it since it first rode through hours earlier.

There were fourteen guns in the trap house and numerous others stashed behind bushes and underneath vehicles all along the block. Marcus had recently been upgraded to the rank of regent for the Dog Pound faction of GDs. He was a ghetto millionaire now, but he wasn't like a lot of rich gangsters who'd paid cash for their rank. He'd earned it through blood, sweat, and tears, through multi-kilo drug distribution and his affiliation with gang wars all across

Chicago's south side neighborhoods. He'd purchased half the guns in his gang's possession, and the other half had been donated by Nya and Grizzy.

The Dog Pound Gangster Disciples were more than ready for war with Bang Boy and his gang of Black P. Stones.

Marcus turned away from the sex scene just as the girl gagged and spit a viscid mouthful of semen onto the bare mattress beneath her. He walked to the living room window and looked out through the blinds. The corners of his mouth rose in an involuntary little smirk as he eyed his cherished Mercedes truck. He'd always wanted a Benz, and now, he had it.

Too bad Grizzy won't be here to shine with me no more, he thought, rolling his black, cotton ski mask down over his face.

It was a heartaching thought, one that instantly ripped away his smirk and replaced it with a cold-eyed mug. Nostrils flaring, he panned his eyes from left to right, looking from corner to corner.

Which was when he saw it — an armored police truck turning onto the block from the north end of Green Street. He glanced to the opposite end of the block just as a second armored truck rounded that corner, followed by a large fleet of CPD cars and SUVs. A light shined down from the sky, and Marcus didn't have to look up to know that the deep thumping noise was the rotor of a police helicopter.

Stumbling backward, he spun away from the window, dropping his cup as he did it. His phone vibrated in his pocket. He ignored it.

"Twelve!" he shouted as he hopped over the threesome on his way to the back door. He took the Glock off his hip and tossed it in a trash can in the kitchen. He snatched the door and rushed out onto the back porch, thinking of the three kilograms of fentanyl-laced heroin he had hidden in the back of a washing machine in the basement.

The thought left him in a hurry because the police were pulling into the dark alleyway when he stepped out onto the porch. He could see another armored truck and two police cars rapidly approaching from the south end of the alley, their high beams lighting the way.

Marcus hurdled the porch railing and landed in the gangway.He immediately climbed the neighbor's eight-foot picket fence and flipped forward over into their neatly arranged backyard, landing hard on his back pockets. He army-crawled to the neighbor's back porch and crawled up onto the splintery, old, wooden steps. He lay flat on his stomach and was knocking at the bottom of the door when, two seconds later, a flood light lit the back porch he'd just escaped.

"Ram the door!" an authoritative voice shouted as a line of police officers in SWAT gear swarmed into the backyard of his trap house.

Marcus wedged his nose between two dirty floorboards and closed his eyes. He didn't move. Didn't breathe. Didn't think. He remained frozen in place for five seconds that could have been five minutes, his heart pounding like the hooves of a raging bull, his fists balled at his sides. He was six feet four inches in height, two hundred sixty pounds of muscle and bone, a large, handsome, Black man who rarely went anywhere without drawing attention, so hiding from droves of trained policemen was a feat.

He heard someone shout, "Chicago Police Department!" The shout was followed by a splintering crash as their battering ram took his back door off its hinges. And at that very same instant, the door next to him was pulled open.

He turned his head toward the door and looked. It was Sheila Cowherd, a fifty-year-old mother of seven and grandmother of nine. Marcus knew this because he knew her entire family. All three of her sons were Dog Pound GDs who were born and raised around Marcus, and he'd dated her second oldest daughter, Shantese, for almost four years. He had two kids by Shantese — his ten-year-old identical twin sons, Marston and Marvell — but he'd never actually entered Miss Sheila's home because the old lady was always flirting with him on Facebook, sending him sexually suggestive memes through Facebook Messenger and leaving heart-eyed emojis in the comments under his pictures.

Right now though, he needed her.

First, she looked out over her fence at the police activity next door. Then, she stared down at Marcus with both her hands planted firmly on her widely sloping hips. She was dressed in a tiny pair of red, booty shorts and a large, red, lace bra, the fabric stretching to accommodate the weight of her massive G-cup breasts. She'd wrapped her hair in an old Fendi headscarf. Her fingernails were manicured — sharp and long and painted blue — and she looked high on something.

"The *hell* you doing on my back porch?" Miss Sheila asked, stretching out the word hell.

"Move. Let me in." Marcus said it urgently and breathlessly, but for one tense moment, Miss Sheila didn't move at all. She merely stared down at him, even as the beam of a flashlight swept her own backyard. Marcus raised the front of his mask, thinking that maybe she didn't recognize him with it on, but she still stared down at him with a scandalous look in her intoxicated eyes.

Finally, she stepped over him, acting as if she was moving closer to the edge of her porch to get a better look at whatever the police were doing, and by the time she turned back to re-enter her home, Marcus was already army crawling past her refrigerator and into the dining room.

"Upstairs," Miss Sheila said, shutting and locking her door. "And be quiet. My drunk ass husband is sleeping off a half gallon of Crown Royal on that couch in the living room."

Marcus moved through the living room on the toe ends of his Nike Air Max '95 sneakers, shooting a quick glance at

Miss Sheila's loudly snoring husband, Crasher, before continuing on to the creaky, old staircase. Andre "Crasher" Cowherd was well known on Chicago's south side, particularly in the Englewood area where he'd established a reputation as one of the most trigger-happy Gangster Disciples the city had ever seen. He and Marcus were around the same age, and though it was no secret that Marcus was a high-ranking GD with long money and a short temper, his name wasn't nearly as feared as Crasher's. Crasher had become so notorious over the years that Englewood natives had started referring to his block, 69th and Paulina, as Crashville. The pot-bellied man was shirtless on the sofa. Four garbage bags that were filled with clothes sat on the floor near one sockless foot.

Marcus gave them no mind as he tiptoed past the sleeping giant and up the steps to the second floor where he quickly locked himself in the small bathroom and took out his iPhone to call Smoke.

No, he couldn't call Smoke, he decided. Smoke and his younger brother, Spazz, had gone to their new home on 69th and Normal, and if the police were raiding Marcus' spot, they were likely raiding Smoke's too.

Marcus had a missed call from Nya. It was the call that came through just as he'd spun away from the window to flee his trap house. Returning the call, he went to the sink and studied himself in the medicine cabinet mirror. There was dirt on the nose of his ski mask, and all over the chest area of his black R.I.P. Grizzy tee, and the front of his black Givenchy shorts. He was dusting it all off when Nya answered the video call.

"Puncho was the other shooter," she said, her words coming out in a great rush. "He's an Undertaker Vice Lord from off Cicero. They say he just left the city."

"Man, twelve just raided my spot," Marcus said, equally rushed. "I made it out the back door just in time. They got a helicopter out here, armored trucks — the whole nine."

"Damn." Nya nibbled at the corner of her bottom lip. "I'm at the hospital. I got hit in a shootout with some of the Undertakers. It's only a thigh wound. Through and through. Doesn't really hurt all that much. I'll be good."

Marcus took off his mask and draped it over the rim of the sink basin. He shut off the light and put his back against the door. The bathroom had a comforting scent to it, like Dove soap and Febreze. He could hear Miss Sheila's heavy footfalls as she ascended the noisy staircase in her fluffy, red slippers. Nya looked like an angel on his phone screen. She showed him the bloodstained bandage on her thigh and the four bad bitches who were standing next to her hospital bed — Quita, Brielle, Niecy, and Noesha. For some reason, Noesha was holding an ice pack to her face.

"Lay low for a day or two," Marcus advised, speaking in a very low whisper. "Take a trip somewhere. We gotta find out what these pigs on. I'm about to write your number down on my forearm just in case I get arrested. They got the whole block surrounded."

"Want me to send somebody to get you?"

"Nah, I'm good. Just do what I said. Lay low. A'ight?"

Nya let out a reluctant sigh and nodded her head. "Don't let up," she said with a clear note of finality in her tone. "We can beat these bitch ass niggas. We got too much money. They can't compete."

Marcus offered her a subtle nod and ended the call as Miss Sheila began twisting the doorknob behind him. He sighed harder than Nya had as he turned to the door and unlocked it. Miss Sheila stepped in, and he closed the door behind her, locking it again. The only light in the bathroom was the home screen of his iPhone. He set it down next to his ski mask and plopped down onto the toilet lid, running his hands down his face. A floodlight spilled in through the window behind the shower curtain, and he inhaled haltingly.

"I knew it was you with that mask on," Miss Sheila said, folding her arms across her enormous melons. "You got the six pointed stars tatted around your elbows. I saw em soon as I opened the door."

Marcus only shook his head. He was listening to the sheer chaos that was taking place all around Miss Sheila's house. He heard the distinctive voices of Fat Folks and Toolie, two of the GDs who'd been posted in the trap house with him, shouting at the arresting officers. Erica Earl, who went by Ree-Ree Folks and lived just across the street from Sheila, was screaming something about the police raiding her house without a warrant. The helicopter sounded closer. Blue and red lights danced across the bathroom window.

"What the hell y'all done did now?" Miss Sheila asked.

"I ain't do shit." Marcus took a pack of Newports out of his pocket and shook one out. Lighting it with his Zippo, he purred and inhaled deeply, ignoring the salacious look Miss Sheila was giving him.

"You're lucky you caught me when I was in the kitchen," she said, moving her hands back to her hourglass hips. "I was just about to grab me a cucumber out that 'frigerator and get busy. I done smoked two blunts to the face and binge watched an hour of C porn. I was about to put that thick ass vegetable to *work*, you hear me?"

She laughed joyously, tossing her head back and smacking her thigh. Marcus didn't react. He puffed his cigarette and leaned back on the toilet, tapping his shoe nervously on the floor. His hands were shaking. His mind was racing. Suddenly, he found himself believing that Nya was as loyal as Grizzy had believed her to be. She wasn't giving him that snake-ish vibe. She'd shot and killed one of the shooters during Grizzy's murder, she'd figured out the identity of the second shooter, and she'd already gotten into a shootout with his gang. She even had her own all-female gang putting in work with her. Surely she hadn't been involved in Grizzy's murder.

So, who was the snake?

The burning hot question was branding itself onto the front of Marcus' mind when Miss Sheila reached out to his crotch and grabbed a handful of his flaccid dick. He flinched, and his first reaction was to grab hold of her wrist and squeeze. But the horny old lady was determined. She didn't let go. In fact, she tightened her grip on the length of his dick and held on.

"Miss Sheila," he said in his most serious tone, "you tweakin."

"No, I ain't. I just told you what I was on before you came knockin' at my door. I was watching C porn. Know what those three letters stand for? Big, black cock. Shantese said you got the biggest dick she ever had, and I want a piece of it."

"Crasher is right downstairs. You can't do folks like that."

"Psshh. My daughter, Lia, just sent me a video of my husband eatin' some stripper's ass at a birthday party last week. It's all over Facebook. You didn't see those bags by his musty ass feet? As soon as he wakes up, his ass is grass, and I'm the lawnmower. Call me Miss John Deere."

Marcus felt his jaw drop a little. At the same time, he heard the harsh static of a police radio somewhere outside the front of Miss Sheila's home. He reacted with a small gasp and a subtle flinch, loosening his grip on Sheila's wrist as the apprehension set in.

And she picked up on the fearful reaction.

"Either you give me some of that dick," she said, letting go of his limp organ and stepping back with her hands on her hips, "or you get the fuck out of my house right now. Ain't no other options."

Marcus' jaw dropped again. Instinctively, he dug in the right-hand pocket of his designer shorts and brought out a twenty-thousand-dollar bundle of hundreds. "Look, I'll pay you for helpin' me out. I got a thousand dollars for you."

"No, you got a thousand dollars to reimburse me for taking those bad ass twins of yours to Six Flags last month and for that school trip to Lincoln Park Zoo me and Shantese just paid for." Sheila slipped her thumbs down into the waistline of her booty shorts and pushed them all the way down to her ankles, and when she stood up, Marcus saw that she wasn't wearing any panties. "I ain't acceptin' nothin' but some dick for helpin' you get away from them police. Either that or I'ma open that window and yell down for them to come up here, black ass."

The hand holding the mound of cash dropped in disbelief. For several seconds, Marcus sat, looking up at Miss Sheila with his head cocked to one side, an incredulous expression etched on his dark hued face.

Sheila Cowherd was far from unattractive. She was a bit on the heavy side, with a single roll of stretch marked fat hanging down around her waist, but her face was gorgeous, and she had a huge yellow ass that always garnered catcalls from the men in their neighborhood. She reminded Marcus of CNN news anchor Sara Sidner — if Sara Sidner was a ratchet grandmother who still dressed like she was twenty. One of her fingernails had broken off on his shorts. She didn't seem to notice. Her eyes were locked on his, and when she saw that he kept glancing at her smoothly waxed pussy, seriously pondering her proposition, she stepped out of the booty shorts and spread her thick legs about two feet apart, rubbing on her clitoris in a slow, circular motion.

Seconds later, with a defeated sigh, Marcus said, "It ain't enough space in this bathroom."

"Come on." Sheila opened the bathroom door. "We can use the guest bedroom. I just cleaned it this morning."

Marcus picked up his phone and ski mask and reluctantly followed her out of the bathroom to a neatly furnished bedroom down the hall. There was a queen-sized bed draped in maroon linen, a new looking dresser with a fifty-inch television standing on it, and two nightstands. There were maroon curtains over the windows and tan colored carpeting.

But it was Miss Sheila's fat, jiggly butt cheeks that had Marcus' undivided attention. She had a tattoo on her left buttock, a salivating tongue sticking out from between a bright red pair of lips. His unwavering gaze was fixed on that lascivious tattoo as Sheila closed the bedroom door, locked it, and climbed onto the foot of the bed. Lowering her head to the goose down comforter, she turned to look over at him, a triumphant smile brightening her yellowish-brown visage.

Downstairs, Crasher was snoring hard and loud. Marcus could hear it clearly. It sounded like an idling chainsaw. He crossed the room to the window, snuck a peek outside, and gasped when he saw that the police had at least eight of his boys in cuffs. The police officers were going in and out of all four houses his gang operated out of. They even had the naked girl who'd worn the bag over her head standing barefoot next to the paddy wagon with a dark colored CPD jacket wrapped around her body, her hands manacled behind her back.

"I can't just fuck you while you got big folks snorin' downstairs," Marcus said as he left the window to stand behind Sheila's fat, yellow derriere. He placed the palm of one hand on her tattoo and shook it, watching the cellulite-filled mass of flesh undulate like waves in Lake Michigan. His dick began to do what it did best when a big-bootied, Black woman was naked before him, throbbing and lengthening and thickening and thumping with the beat of his heart. "I got rid of my pole, and you know if folks come up here and catch me hittin' his wife, he gon' go crazy."

Miss Sheila pointed at the nightstand to her right. "I got a gun in that drawer. It's a four-five. He ain't gon' wake up anyway, but if he does, you'll have that to back his stupid ass up. Just don't kill him."

She crawled forward, her big butt wobbling wonderfully as she moved, and pulled open the drawer herself. She took out a nickel-plated, semiautomatic pistol and backed her wide load to the foot of the bed again. She set the gun down next to her knee and reached back with both hands to pull her mammoth butt cheeks apart.

It was a savory sight. Her pretty pussy spread right open, revealing the enticingly wet pink skin inside it.

"You gon' have to eat this dick first," Marcus said, thumbing down the front of his shorts and liberating his rapidly growing erection. He was a well-endowed man. When fully aroused, his dick measured a few centimeters over eleven inches, and it had a considerable girth. He smacked it on Miss. Sheila's left ass cheek, then the right one, then rubbed the head between her parted labia, fighting off the temptation to slide right into her.

"I don't suck nobody's dick," she told him as she let go of one cheek to fiddle with her clitoris. "I'll tell you what though. You got about five seconds to put your face in this pussy before I start screaming for the police."

Marcus' eyebrows went to his forehead. His lips parted in an open-mouthed smirk. The sheer audacity of Miss Sheila's bold ultimatum momentarily stunned him.

Then, thinking of the chaotic scene he'd just witnessed outside her window, he went down to his knees on the soft, tan carpet and stuck his pointed tongue deep inside Sheila's fat, wet pussy.

Chapter 22

The bed in Nya's private room at the University of Chicago Hospital was much too sumptuous. She didn't even remember closing her eyes. When she opened them and looked at the diamond watch on her wrist, she realized she must have fallen asleep shortly after the FaceTime call with Marcus. The time was 12:41 a.m. She'd taken a short nap and awakened to find that most of her friends had done the same thing. Quita, Brielle, and Niecy were all fast asleep, Quita on Brielle's lap in a cornered armchair with a hospital blanket pulled up on the both of them, Niecy sleeping alone on a rich, leather sofa.

Only Noesha was awake. She was seated under the wall mounted seventy-inch smart TV in a leather chair that looked even more comfortable than the large bed Nya was lying in, sitting back with her meaty legs crossed and her iPhone in hand, the screen light illuminating her gorgeous face as she scrolled through something on the phone.

Nya's phone lay beside her in bed. She picked it up and checked her text messages. She'd received one from Bulletface. It was a video showing him onstage at the MBM concert, holding the mic to his mouth as he spoke to the crowd of crazed fans in front of him.

"I just tried to FaceTime Young Nya," he said, the five diamond necklaces around his neck twinkling brilliantly as he stared down at the camera. The crowd erupted with noise when he mentioned Nya's rap name, bringing an appreciative smile to her face as she sat up in bed and shifted the pillows behind her back. "She ain't answer my call, but I'm sure y'all done heard about what she's goin' through right now. She just lost her husband the other night. She'll be droppin' some new music real soon though. Y'all make some noise for the hottest new female rapper in the game. The queen of drill! Young Nya!"

He turned his back to the crowd and captured video as thousands of elated young Chicagoans went wild behind him. They started a chant. "Nya! Nya! Nya!" Noesha must have looked up and saw the beaming smile on Nya's face because she got up and hurried over to see what she was looking at just as the drumming beat to *Step So Hard* began playing from the speakers inside the stadium.

The video ended as Bulletface was spitting his verse to the song, and Noesha's eyes lit up with excitement.

"Bitch, you really done made it now," she said, not even bothering to use her inside voice for the sake of their sleeping compadres. "You got Bulletface shouting you out on stage. That's next level right there!"

"How's your jaw feeling?" Nya asked the question in a near whisper as she shared the shoutout video to her Instagram page.

"It still hurts a little. That fat fuck must've punched the shit outta me. I don't even remember getting out of the car."

Nya chuckled aloud, fingering her diamond encrusted MBM pendant. The vigorous chuckle caused Quita to stir; Nya only discerned the movement in her peripheral. Her eyes were glued to her phone. She was swiping her way down her long list of new followers, of which there were thousands. *Tens* of thousands. It seemed like she was gaining ten thousand followers every hour.

Two followers in particular caught her eye. The first was Lil Durk, the most popping Chicago drill rap artist alive next to Chief Keef. The second was Young Meach, a platinum-selling Indiana rapper president of Money Bagz Management.

He kept leaving comments under all her posts. Heart eyes and side eyes. Diamonds and eyes. Diamonds and money bags. He had well over thirty million Instagram followers on his page, and despite The Shade Room rumors of him having recently impregnated a famous IG model/Atlanta stripper named Tasia "Baddie Barbie" Olsen, it seemed to Nya that he was only focused on her.

He'd even sent her a direct message. "Hope ur ok. Sorry to hear about ur man. Heard he was a real stepper. Be strong, Young Neezy. Hit my line if you ever need to talk. (219) 555-6390."

Nya's beaming smile expanded. Her heart swelled. She looked up at Noesha's nosey face and discovered a simpering smile that mirrored hers.

"Mmm hmm," Noesha hummed, nodding her head and pointing an accusatory forefinger at Nya's face. "I see who you got eyes on, bitch. You want some of Y.M. in your life. I see. I see."

"You ain't see shit. Mind your goddamn business." Nya shut off her phone screen, snickering guiltily and studying the double Gs on the black, lace, Gucci minidress she'd changed into after the Cicero shootout. She'd purchased a lot of Gucci lately. In her mind, the double Gs stood for Grizzy Gang, and ever since his untimely death, she'd taken a more devoted liking to the high-end designer fashion brand.

Nya's scattered thoughts departed from Lil Durk, Young Meach, and Grizzy when Noesha produced an Apple AirPod from her blue, croc skin, Birkin bag. Sticking to the Hermes haute couture code, she wore a black, leather catsuit by the designer that was cut like fishnets, leaving copious room for her smooth, yellowish-brown skin to breathe in the unforgiving summer heat.

"Did you lose this?" Noesha asked. "I found it in that Cullinan. Right next to the driver's seat."

Nya shook her head and furrowed her brow, staring vacantly at MTN News on the television screen. There was breaking news — two NYPD defectives and an unidentified woman found murdered in a SUV somewhere in Queens, New York. Not that Nya's brain was on the story. She was ruminating over the AirPod Nu-Nu had pinched between a thumb and forefinger.

Then, MTN switched to another breaking story, this one regarding the Highland Park shooting investigation, and Nya's mind went blank when she realized she was looking at live video from the police raids on 72nd and Green. She waved Nu-Nu off, picked up the TV remote, and raised the volume loud enough to awaken her dozing friends. The MTN news reporter was a round faced redbone named Tiffany Roscoe, and she was all business in her canary yellow dress.

"We are live here on the south side of Chicago where police and federal agents have reportedly made numerous arrests related to the Highland Park shooting investigation. Nearly an hour ago, the Chicago Police Department and the ATF launched a massive raid on the gang they believe is responsible for not only the Highland Park massacre but also several other homicides that have taken place on the city's west side this summer. One man — thirty-four-year-old Marcus White, who police say is their chief suspect and the leader of the gang — somehow managed to slip through the perimeter and escape…"

A photo of Marcus appeared on the screen. It showed him and Grizzy leaning back against the trunk of Marcus' slime green Dodge Charger Hellcat, the two of them wearing "Free Larry Hoover" T-shirts with photos of the Gangster Disciple chairman printed on the front. The trunk of the Charger behind them was covered in hundred-dollar bills. Either the police or the news people had blurred out Grizzy's face, but Nya knew her man when she saw him.

"Oh, shit," she murmured, raising her phone to call Marcus.

Noesha shoved Nya's arm down and shook her head. "No. Don't even *think* about calling him. They're trying to charge him with some *west* side murders. You *know* what that means. We need to take his advice and get the fuck outta Chicago."

"She's right," Quita said. She and Brielle were fully awake now, and Niecy was starting to sit up on the sofa.

"Yeah," said Brielle. "We need to go. Let's take a road trip. I've always wanted to do that. We can hop in our trucks and drive down to the A. Rent out a mansion in somebody else's name until we figure out our next move."

Nya was already shaking her head in disagreement.

"Nuh uh. No. Fuck that," she said, raising her phone to dial Lacey's number. "Y'all can leave if that's what y'all wanna do, but I ain't going nowhere until I find Puncho and Bang Boy. It's simple as that."

Chapter 23

Marcus White had eaten his fair share of pussy over the years but never had he done it for so *long*. He'd been at it for more than forty minutes now. His tongue ached, he was glistening wet from his nose down to the collar of his shirt, and he'd ingested more pussy juice than he'd ever swallowed in his life.

It was all Miss Sheila's fault. His dick was as hard as a flagpole, but she didn't want him to stop eating her pussy. She'd already shivered her way through four chin-drenching orgasms, fiddling with her oversized clitoris while Marcus licked and sucked her sweet sugary vaginal lips and squeezed on her ass, and she was working toward a fifth one.

To keep himself from ejaculating prematurely, Marcus blocked out the delicious scent and taste of his former mother-in-law's pussy and focused his thoughts on Lacey. She hadn't texted him in hours — which was unusual to say the least. She was a textaholic, always messaging him accusatory questions about random bitches she'd seen liking or commenting on his social media posts.

Since he no longer suspected Nya of betraying Grizzy, Marcus began to ponder other possibilities. Had Grizzy made the fatal mistake of texting someone his location while they were en route to The Visionary Lounge? Had one of their own gang members revealed to someone that they were heading to the club in Grizzy's flashy, black Rolls Royce

Ghost? And what about Lacey? Had she betrayed Grizzy for a share of that $5 million?

Slurping up another gush of Sheila's tasty vaginal juices, Marcus decided it couldn't have been Lacey. She'd been riding with Nya at the time, and Nya would have seen Lacey texting or calling someone if that were the case.

Miss Sheila yelped and tensed up again. Her big, yellow ass jiggled wildly as she experienced her fifth climax of the hour. Deciding he'd endured enough phallic torture, Marcus stood up and slipped the precum drooling head of his dick right in between her swollen labia.

In St. Charles Boys' School, the juvenile prison he'd spent two years in as a teenager, and also where he'd gotten all his gang tattoos, Marcus had ended most nights sliding his dick in and out of a latex glove filled with lotion that had first been warmed in the microwave. He would wrap a towel tight around the glove to mimic the snugness of a real vagina. The prisoners had called that homemade sex toy a "Fe-Fe," and it had gotten Marcus through the many long nights he'd been forced to spend without the comfort of a Black girl in his bed. Miss Sheila's pussy was just as tight as the fingers in those sexually abused rubber gloves, only her "lotion" was more pleasingly fragrant and didn't require a microwave to maintain its toe-curling warmth, and the added bonus of her fat, bouncing ass and her euphonious little moans brought a smirk to Marcus' handsome face.

For a while, he held her waist in one hand and fucked her senseless, listening more for the motorized snore emanating from the downstairs than the incessant police noises outside. By now, he was convinced he'd gotten away scot free. The police lights were still flashing out there, but the helicopter was gone. The cocktail of drugs in his system dulled his senses, alleviating the fear, slowing his heartbeat, and allowing him to focus all his energy on destroying Sheila's gushing wet pussy.

Which was exactly what he did. For forty-two minutes straight, he pounded in and out of her. His hands were large, black, and replete with veins, and he used them to rub and smack her ass cheeks as she threw it back at him, meeting his every forward thrust. Halfway through, he paused to remove his sweaty shirt and catch his breath, and then, he went at it again, digging in deep, making her squeal.

"This what you wanted, right?" Marcus asked in a low, aggressive tone. He delivered another sharp smack to her right buttock and bit down on the middle of his bottom lip. "Yeah, this it. You wanted me to fuck you just like I used to fuck Shantese, so this what you gon' get ."

In the infamous words of Cardi B, Miss Sheila had some real "wet ass pussy." Her slick vaginal walls gripped his length in a warm embrace, her plentiful juices dripping down onto the comforter below. Wet, sloshing sounds came from inside her. She yelped and seized up as a sixth orgasm shook her to the core, and Marcus was absolutely certain he'd have ejaculated a long time ago had he not eaten a Percocet pill two hours ago.

But the pill could only do so much. Soon, he was digging his fingers into Sheila's hips and shooting gooey ropes of semen deep inside of her tightly gripping vagina. He had a condom in his pocket, but he hadn't thought about it until now, and it was only a fleeting thought. He was far too high to contemplate anything too seriously.

The aftershocks of his orgasm were just starting to wane when he heard the distinctive creak of a floorboard. His eyes went wide and flicked over to the bedroom door, and he was opening his mouth to ask Miss Sheila if she'd heard the same noise when the cheap, wooden doorframe splintered into a thousand shards.

The door swing violently open, and there stood the sleeping giant, only now, he was wide awake and angrier than Tucker Carlson on the day it was announced that Joe Biden had won the 2020 presidential election.

There was a drying sliver of drool on one side of Crasher's fleshy brown face. He was an unattractive man, maybe six-one, at least two hundred eighty pounds, and it was clear that he hadn't visited a gym in years.

His eyes were glossy and crusted at the corners. Exhaling alcohol fumes with every breath he let out, he was a chubby gangster with a beer belly and fat, scarred hands that were currently curling over into fat, scarred fists.

Yanking his shorts over his still twitching phallus, Marcus shifted his gaze to Sheila's pistol, but Crasher rushed at him before he could reach for it, so he knuckled up and swung at Crasher's mouth. The punch landed, but it had little to no effect on Crasher. The big man hammered Marcus with three skull-rocking blows to the face before Marcus could get off another punch, this one a haymaker that struck Crasher somewhere on the side of the head.

Sheila screamed and jumped out of bed as the two large men closed their arms around each other and wrestled around the room, knocking the mattress askew and sending her gun tumbling across the carpet. Marcus lifted Crasher off his feet and slammed him shoulder first into the dresser mirror, the shattering of glass loud and jarring. Sheila screamed again. Marcus winced, afraid that some of the glass would hit him in the face, and Crasher took advantage of the badly timed grimace, spinning off the dresser and picking Marcus up in the same fluid motion.

The rest was a horror-inducing blur. One second, Marcus was airborne, his panic-stricken eyes swinging wildly about the room as he repeatedly drove an elbow down onto Crasher's upper back in an effort to break free. The next second, he captured a flying glimpse of Sheila's undulant backside as she bent over to pick up her pistol. And on the third second, his naked back smashed through the bedroom window, and he went flailing down into the night, his head whipping left and right as the warm summer air enveloped him.

He landed on something hard and flat, and the impact knocked him unconscious.

Chapter 24

Scientists had long alleged that the part of a man's brain that managed his thought process was only active in his waking hours, while a woman's thought process was active even when she slept.

Nya Mixon's thoughts had been a bit fuzzy during her waking hours yesterday, but when she awoke the following morning, she was as clear-minded and cognizant as ever, and during her nine hours of sleep, she'd pieced together all the different threads of evidence and came to a conclusion.

She knew exactly who had betrayed her dearly departed husband.

The sun was a blazing hot ball of unforgiveness when Nya was wheeled out of the University of Chicago Hospital at exactly 10:31 a.m. A nurse pushed her wheelchair through the automatic sliding doors, and Brielle pushed her from there to the open rear passenger's side door of the Rolls Royce Cullinan. Blake had sent an assistant to drive his bloody-seated Bugatti Veyron to a local exotic car dealership for a thorough cleansing, but the two Bentley SUVs that Brielle and Lacey had purchased yesterday were parked right behind the Cullinan.

Nya liked the sight of the three foreign trucks parked back-to-back outside the hospital entrance. She was wearing a pair of Gucci sunglasses with dark lenses, and she'd put on the hood of her black Gucci hoodie and pulled the strings tight to hide her face from the people inside the hospital, but she could see clearly enough to admire the million-dollar trio of SUVs. Four hospital visitors stood just outside the sliding doors with their phones in hand, recording video, taking wild guesses at who the little woman in the wheelchair might be.

"That's Young Nya, ain't it?" One of them guessed as Niecy and Lacey were helping Nya into the hack of the Cullinan.

"Nah, that's Fendi Da Rapper. I'm telling you. That's Fendi."

"It sure ain't Dreezy. She ain't that light skinned."

"Bitch, that's Young Nya. That's her and her Plush Gang squad. Look, that's Lacey's tall ass right there. Look at their chains."

Niecy drove the Cullinan. Noesha sat next to her up front. Quita and Brielle rode in Brielle's Bentayga, and Lacey had her older cousin, Delon, in the passenger's seat of her Bentley truck. He was a tall, brown-hued man with a bald head and gold teeth. The Indianapolis neighborhood he was born and raised in was somewhere on Thirty-sixth Street, so his nickname was Tee Six. Nya had met another man from Nap — a gold-mouthed, dope boy named Carlton "Small Body" Hillman — who'd told her that Tee Six was a rat. He'd told on a murder in prison, and the Gangster Disciples had essentially ostracized him for it. Nya hadn't said anything to Lacey about it because she knew how much Lacey loved her big cousin, but she was going to mention it to her today.

Nya sat alone in the back of the Cullinan, feeling refreshed and full of energy. She sent text messages to her parents, Grizzy's mother, Alvergia, and his daughter, Kamani, letting them all know she was okay and asking how they were holding up. Her mother had already spoken with the realtor. The Arizona mansion was hers once the paperwork was processed. Alvergia and Kamari were grieving, but they were relieved to learn that all the shootings that took place following Lejon's murder were a direct result of his death. At least his gang had retaliated against his enemies; that much had already been confirmed by the superintendent of the Chicago Police Department, who'd stood before an array of news reporters and revealed that a faction of Gangster Disciples had murdered the six men and women in Highland Park because they believed the occupants of the two Sprinter vans were responsible for the murder of Lejon Kamari White. Apparently, someone had given the police some damning information on the Highland Park murders and the names of two of the shooters, including Marcus White, whose slime green Dodge Charger was identified as one of the suspect vehicles.

There was a viral video of Marcus being thrown from a second-floor bedroom window on 72nd and Green. He'd landed right at the feet of the police officers who were searching for him, and the footage was captured live on MTN News. Lacey had shown it to Nya as they were leaving her private hospital room. MTN News reporter Tiffany Roscoe's stunned reaction to the fall was what made the video an instant hit on social media.

Nya took off her hoodie, drew in a deep breath, and let it out, bobbing her head to the melodious tunes of *4Nem*, a new song of hers featuring Is Herbo and Lil Zay Osama that her record label had released at midnight. Niecy had it turned all the way up. Lacey had brought Nya a light brown Gucci jogger to wear home from the hospital, and Nya was wearing her icy MBM chain to accentuate her diamond flooded Patek Philippe watch and the fat eight-carat diamond on her ring finger. Taking her iPhone out of her brown snakeskin Gucci bag and ignoring the argument Noesha and Niecy were having — like Nya, Noesha was an NBA Youngboy fan, and Niecy believed no one in Chicago should listen to Youngboy because of his beef with Lil Durk — Nya decided to keep her opinion to herself and instead composed an Instagram post about Grizzy.

She scrolled through her photo gallery and found one that showed her and Grizzy seated across from each other at GAM's, the Michelin-starred soul food restaurant in downtown Chicago where Grizzy had taken her and their families the day he proposed. The photo showed them regarding each other with the warmest of smiles, Nya clad in the black, silk, Chanel dress he'd bought her for that specific occasion, Grizzy fresh to death in a nice, blue tuxedo over black designer slacks. A single teardrop formed along the lower lid of Nya's left eye as she studied the poignant photo. Then, she blinked, and the tear went skating down her cheek.

"We're up here arguing over some niggas who ain't got a damned thing to do with us," Niecy said, glancing at Nya's disheartened reflection in the rearview mirror as they crossed over into Highland Park. "Meanwhile, our sister's back there crying her goddamn eyes out, and we ain't giving her no kinda attention."

"Nah, don't try to use Nya to get outta this. Be real with yourself. Youngboy's a cold-ass rapper. Just admit it. You can be a Lil Durk fan and still like Youngboy. Shit, I like Cardi B, but Nicki Minaj is still my bitch. I ain't got shit to do with their beef. They both make good music."

The heated dispute brought a simpering smirk to the corners of Nya's pretty mouth. Rolling her equally pretty brown eyes and wiping away the lone tear with the knuckle of her thumb, she said, "I'll settle it once and for all. Lil Durk is the hottest rapper in the industry right now... and so is Youngboy."

Nya knew for certain that her statement would send Niecy through the sunroof, and she couldn't have been more right.

"Ohhh, *please!*" Niecy ranted, nearly swerving into the rear-end of a garbage truck as she shot a fiery glance at the rearview mirror. "This is coming from the bitch who literally *named* herself after Youngboy. Come on now, *Young Nya.* Psshh. What the fuck ever."

Both Noesha and Nya burst out laughing, which only served to bring Niecy's already squinted eyelids even closer together. Nya felt a dull throb in her left thigh, but that was all. The doctor had given her a thirty-day supply of Percocets to help deal with the pain, but she was deathly afraid that the growing fetus in her womb would become addicted to opioids, so she'd only taken half a dose.

Shifting her radiant gaze back to the screen of her phone, she uploaded the photo she'd selected for her Instagram post and began typing out a caption.

"Lejon White. My husband. My king. Who in the city of Chicago stepped harder than you? Nobody. You had these so-called gangstas scared outside, and I'm proud to say that I learned from the best. Watch over me until I get there and tell all those fuck boys who joined you I said hi. Love you, baby. #GrizzyGangForLife."

Nya's smile spanned the entire width of her face as she posted the photo to her Instagram page and shared it to her Facebook and Twitter pages. Altogether, she had over two million followers now. One of her Instagram posts — a video of her and Quita twerking to Latto's *Put It On The Floor* in front of Grizzy's Rolls Royce Ghost — had accumulated over three hundred thousand likes, including likes from Yo Gotti, Chris Brown, and Future, three of her favorite, Black, male celebrities. Latto had also liked and reposted the video. All four of them followed her now.

She left the Instagram app and went to the thread of text messages between her and Money Bagz Management COO and president Demetrius "Young Meach" Burns. He'd sent her his phone number in a direct message on Instagram, and she'd FaceTimed him from the bathroom in her hospital room a little over an hour ago. She'd told him about all the murders she and Grizzy had committed, as well as the ones she'd committed with her girls. She had cried several times during the conversation, and Meach had listened intently, nodding his head here and there, offering small bits of advice, and when she told him who she suspected of betraying Grizzy, he'd helped her cook up the perfect plot to get back at the treacherous snake she had in her circle.

So, she wasn't at all surprised when they arrived at the Highland Park mansion to find Young Meach's MBM tour bus parked in the massive cobblestone driveway out front alongside two snow-white Rolls Royce Spectres and a Phantom Drophead coupe of the same color.

"Ooooh!" Noesha exclaimed, turning in her seat to give Nya a curious little nod. "I see what *you* been up to. You done slid on Y.M. already, huh?"

"Girl, please. My husband *just* died. I wouldn't even *think* of fucking another nigga."

And it was true. Nya's normally hyperactive libido had essentially died with Grizzy. She had no doubt that it would soon return — and likely with a "Hot Girl Summer" vengeance — but right now, sex was the furthest thing from her mind.

She looked back at the crutches she'd gotten from the hospital, considered using them, and then changed her mind and went with the wheelchair. Niecy and Noesha took it out, unfolded it, and rolled it around to her door, and she got out and sat in it by herself, holding her purse close and leaving her hoodie inside the truck.

"On the G," Tee Six said as he got out of Lacey's truck and set his sights on the eight-figure mega mansion, "this some real boss shit right here. I'm actually at Young Nya's mansion. Wait until I tell my lil niggas about this shit. My baby mama ain't stopped playing that song you got with Bulletface since it came out."

He started to raise his smartphone, probably to snap a photo or record a video, but Nya lifted one hand, palm out, the international hand sign for *stop*.

"Nah," she said and took the 40-caliber Glock out of her purse. "No pictures. It's a whole lotta gangsta shit going on over this way. We don't' take too many pictures."

Tee Six's golden smile burgeoned. He wore a white, Fendi jogger, the pants pockets bulging with cash. Two diamond Cuban-links encircled his neck, and a diamond Rolex was on his wrist. He nodded his head understandingly and put the phone back in his pocket.

"I told him not to do that bullshit," Lacey said, scowling at her cousin as she walked past him and joined the rest of the girls surrounding Nya. "I'm sorry about that. I had him come out here, so I can put him back on his feet."

"Yeah?" Nya said tersely. She offered her longtime friend an indifferent shrug, placed the Glock flat on her lap, and turned to Brielle. "Wheel me into the house. They're waiting on me."

"Shit, y'all!" Quita exclaimed, her eyes as wide and round as saucers as she pointed at the ground. There were dozens of wet, red splatters on the clean cobblestone. The trail began at the rear of the Phantom Drophead coupe and led all the way to the front door of the mansion. "That's blood! And it's fresh! Somebody's bleeding in there!"

Two more sets of eyes grew wide with dread. Brielle's and Noesha's. Nya remained stone-faced and told Brielle to continue on. She knew exactly where the droplets of blood had come from. She'd gotten an alert from her Panteon home security app while Lacey was showing her the video of Marcus' viral fall, and she'd watched a few seconds of footage from the exterior PTZ cameras (which stood for pan, tilt, zoom). Two men with blood dripping from their swollen faces had been pulled from the trunk of the Phantom and shoved into the mansion at gunpoint. Nya had smiled at the video before slipping the phone back inside her purse.

The door swung open as they were approaching it, and everyone walking behind Nya froze and gasped when they saw who had opened it.

Alexus Costilla was perhaps the most stunningly attractive, Black woman in all of America. It not, she was certainly close to it. Half African American and half

Mexican, she possessed the face of an angel and the body of a goddess. Her curves were jaw-dropping. Her lashy, green eyes were hypnotizing. Her lips were perfectly shaped and impossibly juicy. Her long, dark hair had a middle part and spilled beautifully down the back of her shoulder-less, white, designer dress, and the many large, flawless, white diamonds around her neck, wrists, and fingers made Nya want to hide hers.

But there was also something notably ugly about Alexus. She had a hot, venomous glare in those sexy green eyes of hers, and her left hand was wrapped tightly around the handle of a gold-plated, fifty-caliber, Desert Eagle pistol with a gold silencer screwed in its barrel.

Eyes asquint, Nya leaned forward to get a better look at the tiny dots on the front of the dress. It was blood, and there was more of it on the toe ends of the billionaire's plain, white, Louboutin sneakers. The tall, heavily muscled, Mexican man standing just behind Alexus was holding a sledgehammer down by his side, and there was even more blood dripping from the business end of it.

Nya tried to swallow but couldn't. Alexus stepped aside, smiling with her mouth and mugging with her eyes, and Nya motioned for Brielle to push her inside.

Brielle hesitated; Nya could feel the subtle vibration of Brielle's shaking hands on the handles of the wheelchair. Finally, after Lacey and Niecy had drawn their own Glock pistols, Brielle moved forward, and they entered the marble floored foyer. Michael Jordan's "23" was emblazoned in the middle of the floor, but no one gave that famous number a second glance.

The two men who'd been pulled from the trunk of the Phantom were seated in wooden chairs to the right of the numbers. Strips of duct tape sealed their mouths shut. Lengths of braided rope bound them to the chairs.

Both men had dreadlocks, and though their faces were beaten beyond recognition, Nya knew who both of them were.

And so did Lacey.

Nya heard the shocked gasp escape Lacey's parted lips. It brought a glorious smile to Nya's face as she spun around to look at her childhood friend. At the same time, Young Meach, Blake, and D-Bay entered the foyer with mini-Dracos cradled in their hands. Blake's 7.62-millimeter pistol was aimed at Lacey, and within two seconds, Meach and D-Bay's were on her too. Alexus took aim at Tee Six.

The two battered and bloodied men were Puncho and Johnny "Bang Boy" Broward, and it was apparent that Bang Boy had taken a number of sledgehammer blows to his right leg. There were far too many angles to that leg, as if it had five different kneecaps that bent in all directions. Glutinous strands of dark red snot dangled precariously from his horribly misshapen nose. A large, round bullet hole graced the knee of his other leg. The pinkie and ring finger of his right hand were gone, and there were thin streams of blood pouring down from the stumps. He was groaning and wheezing, slouched forward against the rope, but at least he was conscious.

Puncho was not. The sledgehammer had shattered the bone below his left eye, and now, the wet eyeball was out of the socket, resting on his cheek like a beach ball on a bungee cord. His loose-fitting Palm Angels shorts looked like they might have been off-white before the assault, but they were too burgundy now to tell for sure.

Raising the Glock pistol from her lap, Nya said, "Nu.-Nu, Niecy, take all their jewelry. Get that gun from Lacey and check her cousin to see if he got one on him."

Noesha and Niecy did as Nya asked, hastily removing the diamond necklaces, bracelets, and watches from Lacey and Tee Six's neck and wrists. Lacey didn't resist when Noesha took the gun from her hand; she appeared to be in genuine shock, staring at Nya with her mouth and eyes agape. Tee Six chuckled drably as his Rolex was being peeled off. "Y'all got all that money and wanna rob a street nigga?"

"You ain't no fuckin' street nigga," Nya said, and she didn't flinch as Alexus aimed and fired off a muted .50-caliber round that turned half of Tee Six's right knee into a fine red mist. He collapsed to the floor immediately thereafter, sitting up with his wounded leg extended before him, and Nya aimed at his forehead. "You told. You snitched on Sparky and Oscar, the two Mexicans who killed an old-school GD they called Payday. Yeah, I know all about that. Your homie, Small Body, told me the whole story."

Tee Six could voice no reply outside of a guttural howl that was not unlike the sound a grizzly bear made when its paw got stuck in the sharp teeth of a bear trap. He clutched worriedly at his gushing leg. Instinctively, Lacey went to his aid, dropping to her knees beside him and giving Nya a confused, frightened look.

"What the hell are you doing, Nya?! This is my *cousin!* Alexus, this is my *family!*

"Why'd you do it, Lacey?" Nya asked coldly. "Why in the fuck you betray Grizzy after all the shit we did for you? Huh? Where's the logic in that? How much did Puncho pay you?! I wanna know."

"And don't lie," Alexus added with a devilishly malevolent little smirk pulling on one side of her mouth, "because he already confessed."

Lacey hesitated. Tiny lakes of salt water sprouted up from her tear ducts and shimmered between her long, faux eyelashes. "I, uhh..."

Lacey hesitated for one second too long, so Alexus shot Tee Six through the nose. It was a macabre thing to see. His head practically exploded like a melon dropped from a seven-story window. Lacey fell back on her hands, which slipped in the blood and sent her sprawling onto her back.

Her small, white, tube top had Plush Gang printed across the chest in red and black lettering, and her white, cotton, booty shorts had the same thing printed on the back; both became soaked and matted to her skin on the places where they'd met the pool of blood.

"I'm sorry!" Lacey shouted, clearly breaking down. "Puncho messaged me on Facebook, asking to hang out with me. The nigga wanted to eat my ass, let me sit on his face, suck my toes. It just sounded too good. I swear. That's how it happened. I know he's ugly as shit, but I was horny, and I had money to blow, so I went. I got a hotel suite and gave him the location, and when he got there, he flipped the script. Got to asking me about Grizzy, asking if I knew where to find him. He offered to pay me fifty bands if I could get him close to Grizzy, so he could kill him."

"And you *accepted* it?" Nya asked, unable to contain her fury. She stood from the wheelchair, shifting her weight to her right leg and tightening her grip on her Glock. "You sold him out for fifty thousand dollars?!"

"No!" Lacey struggled to her feet, wiping the wet palms of her hands on the front of her shorts. She looked from Nya to Alexus and back to Nya again. She flexed her manicured fingers nervously. "Okay, listen. I told him I wanted a million dollars if I was going to help him. He claimed that wouldn't leave him with anything, and I said bullshit. I knew that Bang Boy had put $5 million on Grizzy's head. That surprised him. U.T. had told him somebody had offered $1 million. Then, Puncho agreed to pay *me* $1 million and... I'm so sorry. I helped him. I was on the phone with him when we left out for the show."

"I know," Nya said, nodding her head as it all came together in her mind. "You had an AirPod in your ear, and you dropped it in the truck, didn't you?"

"Oh, shit!" Noesha exclaimed, her brow rising as she realized the AirPod she'd found in the Cullinan belonged to

Lacey and that Lacey had used it to communicate with Grizzy's killer.

"I'm so sorry, Nya." Lacey was full-on sobbing now. She buried her face in the palms of her hands. "I wasn't thinking. Marcus was in my ear. He kept saying we deserved more than y'all gave us. I'm so sorry, Nya. I swear to God. If I could take it all back, I would."

Nya didn't accept the apology. She'd been best friends with Lacey ever since they were kids, and not once had she even contemplated betraying their friendship.

"Tick tock," Alexus said, tapping a forefinger on her one-of-a-kind Richard Mille wristwatch. "I do have plans, you know. You need to decide what you're gonna do with her."

A life-or-death ultimatum from the world's wealthiest person. The most followed woman on social media. It was surreal. Nya looked over at Alexus, admiring the big, round ass, the narrow waist, and the huge, perky tits that were all wrapped tightly in the form fitting, Versace dress. Her gorgeous, reddish-brown visage was framed by waist-length, black hair that was as straight as thread; the fat, square diamond in a necklace and bracelet set must have cost at least $2 million. Nya had seen the huge Mexican bodyguard with Alexus before. He was always with her when she was on the red carpet, or leaving a restaurant, or posing for photos with fans. They called him Bojo, and despite the recent rumor that Alexus had been creeping around with him behind Blake's back, he'd kept his job as the main protector of a woman whose net worth now well exceeded $225 billion.

Blake was just as icy as his wife. There were no Cuban-links for him. There was just one necklace with enormous, round-cut, white diamonds, a few icy rings, and a deco translucent green Richard Mille watch that had no diamonds but probably cost at least $3 million. His teeth were covered in diamonds, and he was tall, dark, handsome, and muscular, just like Grizzy had been. Alexus was one lucky woman.

Swinging her gaze back over to Lacey, Nya raised her black Glock. She lined up the sights with the center of Lacey's forehead.

"Nuh uh," Quita said.

"No, no, no," Niecy said, bringing her hands together in prayer as her pretty eyes filled with tears.

Alexus walked over to stand beside Nya. She was 5'7", but next to Nya, she looked 6'0". The aromatic perfume she was wearing made Nya's mouth water. Nya was no lesbian, but she had a huge crush on Queen A. She was starstruck, and she found it difficult to look at Alexus without fantasizing about going down on her.

It's the money, Nya thought to herself. *She's worth over $200 billion, and she's a bad mixed bitch with a fat ass. Who wouldn't find her attractive?*

All of Nya's friends were in tears. It was an emotional moment. Nya eased her finger over the trigger. Inhaled. Exhaled.

"You broke the code, Lace. Grizzy was the love of my life, the man who put us all in this position to win, and you got him killed." She shook her head. "I can't forgive you for that."

Lacey's frantic, gaping eyes flicked over to Noesha. "Don't let them do this to me, Nu-Nu. We're Plush Gang. We go too far back for it to end like this. Please. Plea…"

This time, it was Lacey's head that practically exploded. Nya flinched at the low, dull *Pyoo!* of the high caliber round exiting the huge barrel of Alexus' gold-plated Desert Eagle. Noesha screamed, Niecy flinched and turned away, Quita and Brielle flinched and *ran* away toward the lavishly furnished sitting room, and Nya, shifting her attention to Puncho's brutally beaten figure, limped over to him and pressed her Glock to the side of his face that wasn't caved in.

"Hey. Mr. Puncho. You still alive?" She nudged him with the gun barrel.

A sickeningly wet inhalation of air was Puncho's response, and a rapid burst of fully automatic gunfire from the modified Glock 23 was Nya's. It was an instant death. His skull broke apart like an egg and emptied onto the floor beside him.

The gunshots brought Bang Boy to a more alert state of consciousness. He let out a long, miserable groan. "I'm... I nee... help," he muttered, raspy.

The sticky sound of bloody footfalls ensued as Alexus sauntered over to stand beside Nya. At the same time, Noesha and Niecy ran from the foyer to join Quita and Brielle in the sitting room, while three more huskily built Hispanic men emerged from an elevator down the east hall wearing white biohazard suits and pushing a large, steel cart with rubber gloves, body bags, and cleaning chemicals on the shelves.

"They needed to see that," Alexus said, scowling down at Bang Boy. "Your friends, I mean. It'll keep them in line. Dissuade them from betraying us in the future." She put an arm around Nya's shoulder and hugged her close "You might wanna rethink killing this one. He may be more important to you than you know."

"Nuh uh." Nya pressed the hot barrel of her pistol against Bang Boy's forehead and pushed until his swollen black eyes were fixed on her furious, red-veined ones. "This motherfucker will never be important to me."

"You sure about that?" Alexus asked.

Nya turned to look at Alexus just as the impossibly beautiful woman turned to look at her. There was a look in Alexus' eyes, some sort of game changing revelation. Slowly, Nya narrowed her eyes, tilted her head to one side, and stared up at the most famous woman on the planet.

"You know something I don't know?" Nya asked after a time.

"I had Bojo do some research on this guy," Alexus said with a gentle nod, "right before he flew out to the Big Apple to get rid of those two nasty detectives and the fat chick who was threatening to rat on Johnna Broward. I had Bojo check into the whole beef between this guy here and your old man, Grizzy. Come to find out, they had somewhat of a sibling rivalry. Cain and Abel you might call it."

Nya furrowed her brow as Young Meach rolled her wheelchair over and helped her lower herself back into the seat. Was Alexus saying what Nya thought she was saying?

"Yeah," Alexus said, reading her mind. "Willie White and April Broward were sleeping around behind Alvergia's back. Had two kids right under her nose. Johnna and Johnny. They both share the same biological father as your husband."

Nya's lower jaw divorced her upper one, and her lips parted with an audible smack. Looking at Bang Boy now with his head all lumped up and puffy, his eyes nearly swollen shut, and his dreadlocks dripping blood all over his designer shirt, it was difficult to discern any notable similarities between him and Grizzy but thinking back to the Instagram videos she'd seen of Bang Boy since his release from prison, she could see the resemblance. Both Grizzy and Bang Boy were tall and dark and incredibly well-muscled. They had the same facial structures, the same alpha male mentalities. And both of them had been raised by Willie White.

Alexus was still talking. It was something about Nya not having to worry over any neighbors complaining to police about the gunfire, that the mansion had been soundproofed specifically because of the Matamoros Cartel's propensity for murder, but Nya hardly even heard the words. She was in a state of shock and disbelief.

The man who was responsible for her husband's death was the uncle to her unborn child.

Alexus placed a supportive hand on Nya's shoulder. "Don't worry about the loss of your friend back there," she said, her malevolent tone shifting to a much more benevolent one. "You've gained a new one. You're signed to Blake's record label, and I'm already in business with Johnna Broward. It'd be much better if we just came together and focused on getting money. I doubt if Bang Boy will be causing you any more trouble. You've killed the man who killed your husband, and although you were too friendly to pull the trigger on Lacey, you had a real bitch like me to do it for you. I say we join forces. You'll become a part of the *real* money team. The Billionaire Girls' Club."

Bang Boy coughed once. A mist of red sprayed from between his busted-up lips and landed on Nya's jogger. She looked down in disgust as the spats of blood soaked into the fabric of her pants. Meach rolled her backwards. He guided her away from the carnage and pushed her into the sitting room where her girls gathered. All four of them turned to look at her, their expressions a diverse array of bottomless grief, paralyzing shock, and infinite heartache.

Nya stood up and limped over to the white, leather sofa, settling down next to Quita and tucking her Glock inside her purse. All eyes remained on her, but she took a moment to get her thoughts together before she spoke. While she did that, Meach took her wheelchair back to the foyer, and when Nya looked that way, she saw that one of the cleaners was busy bleaching away the blood from the wheelchair's tire treads while the other cleaners zipped Lacey Carter's unmoving corpse into a white body bag.

"I don't like what happened," Nya said finally, her gaze wandered the room from one despondent set of eyes to the next. "But it had to end that way. Y'all understand that, right?"

Noesha was the first to nod her head, her vacant stare fixed on Lacey's Cuban-link necklace and the attached Plush Gang pendant that she held in her closed fist. Everyone else followed suit. Nya was ready to say more, but Alexus entered the room before she could say it. Alexus had taken off her bloody Christian Louboutin sneakers and the blood-stained

Versace dress. Her flawless body was revealed in her white, lace, Savage X

Fenty bra and thong panties set.

"Hand me that," Alexus said, reaching for the Plush Gang necklace Noesha was holding.

Noesha looked to Nya, who spent several seconds thinking it over. Alexus was the world's richest person, but that had very little to do with Nya's decision to nod her head yes. It was the fact that Alexus and her father's family had all been arrested and charged with running one of Mexico's most ruthless drug cartels, and none of them had snitched, which ultimately led to their acquittals. It was the fact that Alexus was married to Bulletface, the mouthwateringly handsome, Black man who was perhaps the most gangster rap artist to ever live, the man who'd taken what rap greats like Boosie and Jeezy had done and rocketed it to another level. Nya respected a person who could endure the heat of the streets and keep their lips sealed when the police caught up with them, so she nodded her head and regarded Alexus with a sinister little smirk, and Noesha handed over the chain and pendant. Quita helped Alexus put it on.

"No snitching, no freezing up, and no turning on the gang," Nya said to Alexus. "I know you already abide by that code, but that's what it means to be a Plush Gang member."

"I'm all in," Alexus said. "I'm with Blake everywhere he goes anyway, and I don't have a lot of girlfriends I can hang out with every day. I'll just make sure you're on tour with Blake from now on, and we can all kick it together backstage before your performances."

There were smiles all around. Nya sighed, and it felt like the weight of the world fell from her shoulders when she exhaled.

She took out her phone and went to the photo gallery. She spent twenty seconds studying all the recent photos and videos of her late husband.

"We won the war, baby," she whispered under her breath. "We won."

EPILOGUE

September 29, 2023

The not-so-comely effects of pregnancy were beginning to set in. Nya's feet were swollen, so she could no longer wear her high-heeled shoes around the house. She hadn't experienced any morning sickness, but her appetite had taken a dramatic turn for the strange and unsavory, and now, she had an insatiable craving for Doritos drenched in Hershey's chocolate syrup, sixteen-ounce steaks covered in mustard and Louisiana hot sauce, and peanut butter coated honey buns. The result was an additional twenty pounds of weight that seemed to have gone straight to her breasts, ass, and thighs, and when she started feeling too heavy, she began visiting the gym on the fifth floor of the building she now lived in.

She'd moved to Atlanta and lived in a five-million-dollar condo in the affluent Buckhead section of town. She'd bought a matte black Rolls Royce Spectre to get around in, and she'd hired Brielle as her driver. Niecy was her assistant, in charge of managing her busy itinerary and keeping track of her doctor's appointments. Noesha was her publicist and social media director, which meant she was the one who snapped all the photos while Nya was in the studio or when she was performing live onstage in front of thousands of concert goers. Quita had no official occupation, but she and her two sisters, Iyanna "Lulu" Hales and Kayota "Mook" Hales, were putting the finishing touches on a two-million-dollar brick-and-mortar business near the Buckhead Village shopping district that would include a hair and nail salon, a health and fitness spa, and designer clothing store. Nya had purchased the building with $830,000 from her checking account and used over $1 million of the drug money she got from Blake to finance the renovations.

Steppers, Young Nya's first official album, was released on the fourth of August, and it was certified platinum five days later. Her album sales were fueled by a Chicago Sun Times article that alleged Nya and her Plush Gang clique were the main suspects in a slew of west side murders that had taken place over the summer. Add to that the many other hot rap and R&B recording artists who'd collaborated on eleven of the nineteen songs with Nya — veterans like Bulletface, Future, Young Meach, Bump J, and Sly Polaroid, exceedingly gorgeous female emcees Megan Thee Stallion, Cardi B, Dreezy, the Trap Twinz, and the City Girls, fellow Chicago natives Lil Durk, Lil Zay Osama, Fendi Da Rapper, Jeremih, and the DCT Brothers, and soulful R&B artists Mary J. Blige, Alicia Keys, Coco Jones, and Queen Naija — and her debut album was destined for success. Her hit single, *Step So Hard*, featuring Bulletface had risen to double platinum status and garnered an all-girls remix featuring the Trap Twinz, Flomilli, and Sexyy Red that was certified gold within four days of its release.

Young Nya's live performances were just as lit. She'd completed the last leg of the MBM Tour with Bulletface and her other labelmates, raking in $75,200 off each of the remaining nineteen stadium concerts, including two sold out shows at Madison Square Gardens and three at the United Center, and she'd done an additional twenty-two solo shows that had paid her an additional average of $184,900 per performance.

Alexus had purchased brand-new, diamond-encrusted Plush Gang pendants for every member of the clique that cost upwards of $300,000 apiece — and she'd also paid for

Nya's transportation to every concert venue in a sparkling fleet of snow-white Rolls Royces, Bell helicopters, and Gulfstream private jets, making it a breeze for Nya to travel to and from her Atlanta home to football and basketball stadiums nationwide.

Nya had performed again tonight, Friday, September 29th. It was the last stop on her own Plush Gang tour, a sold-out show at the Lucas Oil Stadium in Indianapolis, Indiana. She'd had a long list of surprise guests: Bulletface and the whole MBM squad, including Young Meach, who'd used every gesture in the book of love to impress her, Fendi Da Rapper, GloRilla, Dreezy, Gloss Up, Lil Durk, Kodak Black, Lil Baby, Moneybagg Yo, Polo G, Gucci Mane, Yo Gotti, EST Gee, Latto, and Megan Thee Stallion; and even Mary J. Blige, the legendary queen of R&B.

Subconsciously, Nya felt uneasy about performing while pregnant. But the people wanted her, so she came out and performed every day and night, canceling only one show when she'd sprained her ankle onstage at the State Farm Stadium in Glendale, Arizona three weeks ago.

When the Gulfstream 650 that she and her girls had flown to Indianapolis and returned to Atlanta took off, Nya was fast asleep beneath a dark blue, Gucci blanket. She'd had Grizzy's face airbrushed across the middle of it. She'd changed clothes eight times during her performances, and the black and gold Chanel cocktail dress she wore now was her last wardrobe change. She'd taken her son along with her this time; he, too, was asleep, curled up on Niecy's lap with his fingers closed around his plastic John Cena action figure.

Quita awakened Nya by flicking the tip of her nose.

Nya's eyes popped open, and she shot Shaquita Hales a stern, sleepy look.

Quita laughed. "Come on, sis. We're here. And you got company."

"Don't get beat up," Nya threatened. Yawning, she turned to look out her window. There was a black Ferrari SUV parked behind Alexus' all-white fleet of Rolls Royces. The headlights were on. A tall man on crutches approached the jet with a brown-skinned woman walking alongside him. "Is that him?"

Quita nodded. "Him and his girlfriend, Shanelle. She used to be an officer at that fed joint he was locked up in."

Nya sighed and rose from her seat. She stretched and worked the kinks out of her neck. This would be her first time seeing Johnny Broward in person since the day she'd come close to murdering him inside Alexus and Blake's Highland Park mansion. She didn't know how to approach him. Part of her wanted to blow his brains out. Grizzy would still be alive and well had Bang Boy not put that $5 million on his head.

In Bang Boy's defense, he had apologized repeatedly over the past couple of months, especially after he and his sister took the DNA tests that confirmed Willie White had fathered both him and Johnna. His mother had broken down and confessed to the scandalous affair. She and Grizzy's mother, Alvergia "Ne-Ne" White, had been close friends for years. In fact, it had been Ne-Ne who first introduced April to her husband, Johnathan "Big Johnny" Broward, a construction carpenter from Rockford, Illinois, and April had selfishly taken advantage of that friendship by sleeping around with Ne-Ne's husband.

Johnna Broward was already capitalizing off the story, milking it for all it was worth. She'd done an entertainingly dramatic interview on MTN's *The Rita Mae Bishop Show*, spilling all the tea. "So, now I learn that my favorite new female rapper is pregnant with my long-lost brother's baby, and my childhood friend, Alaina, is actually my biological sister," she'd said through a face full of tears. According to the New York Times, she was already in talks with a major publisher. She was going to write a memoir about the whole ordeal.

As Nya and her four besties were gathering their things to exit the private jet, she couldn't help by wonder what Johnna was going to do if it was ever revealed that she'd been under federal investigation for allegedly jumpstarting Panteon Technologies with the drug proceeds Willie White's gang of Black P. Stones had accumulated before they were indicted.

Not that it ever *would* get out. Alexus had told Nya everything about the potentially career-ending situation she'd handled for Johnna. Bojo, Alexus' ogre-sized bodyguard, had popped up in New York City and murdered some NYPD detective named Rick McKenzie as he sat at his dining room table. Then, Bojo had taken McKenzie's partner, Erica Sinclair, hostage and forced her to take him to pick up Diana Martin-Caldwell, the woman who'd been scheduled to meet with the FBI to reveal everything she knew about Johnna Broward's illegitimate financial dealings. He'd shot and killed Diana and then had killed the lady detective to tie up the loose ends.

That had ended the federal probe into Johnna Broward and Panteon Technologies.

There was a sweltering humidity in the air when Nya descended the steps of the Gulfstream jet with her own personal bodyguard leading the way. His name was Timothy Williams, but everyone called him BD Black because he was a member of the Fifth Ward Black Disciples, and his complexion was charcoal black. He was tall, heavyset, and vigilant, and Nya hiring him had everything to do with his criminal history. He'd just come home from serving twenty-one years in prison for a murder. His gang had vouched for him. He was a real street nigga who'd never snitched on anyone, and Nya had hired him after a fan got too close while she and the girls were out shopping one day in Buckhead Village.

Bang Boy stood next to the staircase and stared up at Nya as she moved closer to him. She tried to gauge his attitude and came up with nothing.

He was clean as fuck and iced out. The long muscles in his powerful arms flexed as he gripped the crutches on either side of him.

Nya glanced down at the brand-new, titanium iPhone 15 Pro Max in her hand. Instagram was still on her screen. She almost smiled at the number of followers she'd gained over the past three months. She was up to nine million now. Many of them were A-list celebrities. She'd just uploaded a video to her Instagram stories, giving her opinion on Duane "Keefe D" Davis being arrested earlier today for the 1996 murder of Tupac Shakur. The video already had more than three million views.

Nya had a Glock 33 in the Hermès Birkin purse hanging down from her left shoulder. She briefly considered taking it out. She had faith in her team, but there was no one on Earth she trusted more than herself. She turned her head and shot a quick glance over her shoulder, as if merely checking to see that Niecy was carrying Quendell down the steps behind her, but in all actuality, she was looking to see who was on point.

She found what she was looking for in Noesha. The thickly built yellow bone's hand was buried in her oversized Gucci shoulder bag where her fully automatic Glock pistol resided, and her cool green eyes were glued to Bang Boy and his girlfriend.

Snapping her gaze back to Bang Boy, Nya put on a fake smile and gave him a wave.

Bang Boy's smile looked just as fictitious.

"There she is," he said, beaming. "Young Nya in the flesh. I don't know if I should be asking for an autograph or asking about the baby."

Nya chuckled once, and Bang Boy fell in step beside her as they headed toward their vehicles.

"Just watched that video you posted talking about Keefe D," he said, swinging his crutches forward on the asphalt. "I agree with you. That nigga told on his goddamn self. Dumbass."

Nya nodded her head. BD Black pulled open the rear door of one Rolls Royce Phantom and stepped aside, so she could climb in.

"Get in and talk with me for a second," Nya said to Bang Boy.

Shanelle gave him a look, but he handed his crutches over to her and slipped in next to Nya, wincing against the pain it caused him to scoot across the sumptuous, white, leather seat.

Meanwhile, Niecy set Quendell's sleeping figure in his car seat in the back of the Phantom that was parked just behind the one Nya was in, while Brielle and Quita lingered just outside Nya's open door, discussing how they were to see Beyoncé's Renaissance film when it debuted in December. BD Black stood in the Black Disciple stance — fingers interlaced on his fat, round belly, thumbs pressed together in a kind of pyramid — with his dark, calculating eyes locked on Bang Boy. Shanelle was on her phone, scrolling through something.

"Close the door, Black," Nya said, and she kept her eyes on Bang Boy as the suicide door swung shut beside him. He was still wincing a little, so she asked, "Are you okay?"

Bang Boy nodded, but there was an immense pain on his face. He had on a stylish, black and red, Givenchy T-shirt over black Amiri jeans and black and red Jordan sneakers. His neck, wrists, and fingers were replete with flawless, white diamonds... the fingers he had left.

"It'll pass in a minute," he said through clenched teeth. "It must be about to rain. Every time it's about to storm, these broken bones start to aching."

"You know," Nya said, "I had no idea Alexus was really a gangsta until that day. I had heard all the cartel rumors, but I thought that was just another made-up story. Like the one they made up about Ciara, saying she was born a man. Or the one about Durk, when they said he had got choked out by Lil Reese. Niggas just be making shit up. I mean, I do remember seeing that video of Alexus shooting at Blake's tour bus, but he had just cheated on her. I probably would've done the same thing."

"Her bodyguard caught me in the restroom at a gas station out south. I was taking a piss. That big ass nigga knocked me out and pushed me out the side window to some other Mexicans, and they put me in the trunk of that drop-top Phantom with Puncho."

Nya thought back to that day, and the grief she'd been going through at the time resurfaced. She gave Bang Boy a squinted side eye.

"I hope you know I'll never be able to fully forgive you for that shit," she said after a time. "You took a piece of my heart when you took Grizzy from me. I loved that man more than I loved myself."

"How the fuck you think I feel? You think I would've put that money on his head if I knew he was my blood brother? I gotta look myself in the mirror everyday knowing I not only got my brother killed but also that I got my *father* killed in prison. That shit ain't stopped bothering me yet. I was just telling Shanelle this morning how Willie practically *raised* me out there in the Gardens. Kept me by his side every day. He was the reason I became a Stone in the first place. I never even had a clue that he was my real daddy. Johnna didn't know either. Shit, I'm not even sure *he* knew. I went to war with the Dog Pound GDs when I was a shorty, whacked a couple of them niggas, and none of that shit would've happened had I known that Grizzy was my whole fuckin' *brother*."

The burgeoning tears in Bang Boy's eyes left little doubt that he was being truthful. He sniffled to hold back the tears. He grimaced against the ache in his bones, shook his head, and scratched at the outside of his forearm.

"On Jeff Fort," he said, clenching his teeth again, "I sincerely apologize for what happened to your husband — what happened to *my brother*. I'm sorry as fuck about that. But all that's history now. Ain't shit we can do but move on."

"You don't have any medicine for the pain?" Nya asked, her brow wrinkled with concern.

He shook his head and muttered something about having left his medication at his home in California, so Nya dug around in her purse and came out with a bottle of Percocets. She unscrewed the cap, shook a few of them out onto her open palm, and handed them to Bang Boy. He popped one immediately and gulped it down without water.

"My sister told me you hung out with her the other week," he said. "She really appreciates that shit. I know she's rich as fuck, but she's still just a girl from the projects, and she ain't really got a whole lot of celebrity friends. She couldn't stop talking about that party you had after that concert. She said just about every Black celebrity in the industry was there."

Nya nodded and smiled at the memory. Following her own sold-out show at Atlanta's Mercedes-Benz Stadium, she had thrown a birthday party for Noesha at a thirty-million-dollar mega mansion in Douglasville, Georgia, and half of Black Hollywood had shown up for the celebration. Johnna had gone home with Quavo of the Migos; earlier today, TMZ had reported that Johnna Broward and Quavo were rumored to be dating, making it the biggest dating headline since Taylor Swift and Travis Kelce.

"Just be there for my son when he gets here," Nya said, glancing at her watch for the time. "Be a good uncle. But look, I gotta get home. Call me tomorrow. We'll go out for lunch if you're still here in the A."

Bang Boy gave her a nod and a subtle smile. He knocked on his window, and BD Black pulled it open and helped him over to his crutches. Bang Boy stumbled, but Shanelle quickly helped him find his footing. She held his elbow and walked him to the passenger's door of his Ferrari SUV. Nya watched them closely.

BD Black and the girls went back on the jet to grab all their luggage as Shanelle and Bang Boy were pulling off, and approximately seven minutes later, Nya and her gang departed the airport in three white Rolls Royce Phantoms. They passed Bang Boy's blacked-out Ferrari Purosangue on their way back to Nya's spacious Buckhead condo. It was parked on the side of the road with the hazard lights blinking, and there were two Atlanta police cars and an ambulance parked just ahead of it. Shanelle was running alongside a stretcher two medics were rolling toward the open rear doors of the ambulance, and Bang Boy's limp body was laid out on the stretcher.

A sinister little smirk formed at one corner of Nya's pretty mouth as she looked down at the bottle of pills in her purse. It was the same pill bottle she was given when she was shot in the thigh nearly three months ago, only the twelve pills were different.

The Percocets inside the bottle were made of pure fentanyl!

The End.

Lock Down Publications and Ca$h Presents
Assisted Publishing Packages

BASIC PACKAGE $499 Editing Cover Design Formatting	**UPGRADED PACKAGE** $800 Typing Editing Cover Design Formatting
ADVANCE PACKAGE $1,200 Typing Editing Cover Design Formatting Copyright registration Proofreading Upload book to Amazon	**LDP SUPREME PACKAGE** $1,500 Typing Editing Cover Design Formatting Copyright registration Proofreading Set up Amazon account Upload book to Amazon Advertise on LDP, Amazon and Facebook Page

***Other services available upon request.
Additional charges may apply

Lock Down Publications
P.O. Box 944
Stockbridge, GA 30281-9998
Phone: 470 303-9761

Submission Guideline

Submit the first three chapters of your completed manuscript to ldpsubmissions@gmail.com. In the subject line add **Your Book's Title**. The manuscript must be in a Word Doc file and sent as an attachment. Document should be in Times New Roman, double spaced, and in size 12 font. Also, provide your synopsis and full contact information. If sending multiple submissions, they must each be in a separate email.

Have a story but no way to send it electronically? You can still submit to LDP/Ca$h Presents. Send in the first three chapters, written or typed, of your completed manuscript to:

LDP: Submissions Dept
P.O. Box 944
Stockbridge, GA 30281-9998

DO NOT send original manuscript. Must be a duplicate. Provide your synopsis and a cover letter containing your full contact information.

Thanks for considering LDP and Ca$h Presents.

NEW RELEASES

BLOODLINE OF A SAVAGE 1&2
THESE VICIOUS STREETS
RELENTLESS GOON
RELENTLESS GOON 2
BY PRINCE A. TAUHID

THE BUTTERFLY MAFIA 1-3
BY FUMIYA PAYNE

A THUG'S STREET PRINCESS 1&2
BY MEESHA

CITY OF SMOKE 2
BY MOLOTTI

STEPPERS 1,2&3
BY KING RIO

THE LANE 1&2
BY KEN-KEN SPENCE

THUG OF SPADES 1&2
LOVE IN THE TRENCHES 2
BY COREY ROBINSON

TIL DEATH 3
BY ARYANNA

THE BIRTH OF A GANGSTER 4
BY DELMONT PLAYER

STEPPERS 3 | KING RIO

PRODUCT OF THE STREETS 1&2
BY DEMOND "MONEY" ANDERSON

NO TIME FOR ERROR
BY KEESE

MONEY HUNGRY DEMONS
BY TRANAY ADAMS

Coming Soon from Lock Down Publications/Ca$h Presents

IF YOU CROSS ME ONCE 6
ANGEL V
By Anthony Fields

IMMA DIE BOUT MINE 4&5
By Aryanna

A THUGS STREET PRINCESS 3
By Meesha

PRODUCT OF THE STREETS 3
By Demond Money Anderson

CORNER BOYS
By Corey Robinson

SON OF A DOPE FIEND 4
By Renta

THE MURDER QUEENS 6&7
By Michael Gallon

CITY OF SMOKE 3
By Molotti

BETRAYAL OF A G
By Ray Vinci

CONFESSIONS OF A DOPE BOY
By Nicholas Lock

THA TAKEOVER
By Keith Chandler

Available Now

RESTRAINING ORDER 1 & 2
By **CA$H & Coffee**

LOVE KNOWS NO BOUNDARIES 1-3
By **Coffee**

RAISED AS A GOON I, II, III & IV
BRED BY THE SLUMS I, II, III
BLAST FOR ME I & II
ROTTEN TO THE CORE I II III
A BRONX TALE I, II, III
DUFFLE BAG CARTEL I II III IV V VI
HEARTLESS GOON I II III IV V
A SAVAGE DOPEBOY I II
DRUG LORDS I II III
CUTTHROAT MAFIA I II
KING OF THE TRENCHES
By **Ghost**

LAY IT DOWN I & II
LAST OF A DYING BREED I II
BLOOD STAINS OF A SHOTTA I & II III
By **Jamaica**

LOYAL TO THE GAME I II III
LIFE OF SIN I, II III
By **TJ & Jelissa**

IF LOVING HIM IS WRONG...I & II
LOVE ME EVEN WHEN IT HURTS I II III
By **Jelissa**

STEPPERS 3 | KING RIO

BLOODY COMMAS I & II
SKI MASK CARTEL I, II & III
KING OF NEW YORK I II, III IV V
RISE TO POWER I II III
COKE KINGS I II III IV V
BORN HEARTLESS I II III IV
KING OF THE TRAP I II
By **T.J. Edwards**

WHEN THE STREETS CLAP BACK I & II III
THE HEART OF A SAVAGE I II III IV
MONEY MAFIA I II
LOYAL TO THE SOIL I II III
By **Jibril Williams**

A DISTINGUISHED THUG STOLE MY HEART I II &
III
LOVE SHOULDN'T HURT I II III IV
RENEGADE BOYS 1-4
PAID IN KARMA 1-3
SAVAGE STORMS 1-3
AN UNFORESEEN LOVE 1-3
BABY, I'M WINTERTIME COLD 1-3
A THUG'S STREET PRINCESS 1&2
By **Meesha**

A GANGSTER'S CODE 1-3
A GANGSTER'S SYN 1-3
THE SAVAGE LIFE 1-3
CHAINED TO THE STREETS 1-3
BLOOD ON THE MONEY 1-3
A GANGSTA'S PAIN 1-3
BEAUTIFUL LIES AND UGLY TRUTHS
CHURCH IN THESE STREETS
By **J-Blunt**

STEPPERS 3 | KING RIO

PUSH IT TO THE LIMIT
By **Bre' Hayes**

BLOOD OF A BOSS 1-5
SHADOWS OF THE GAME
TRAP BASTARD
By **Askari**

THE STREETS BLEED MURDER 1-3
THE HEART OF A GANGSTA 1-3
By **Jerry Jackson**

CUM FOR ME 1-8
An LDP Erotica Collaboration

BRIDE OF A HUSTLA 1-3
THE FETTI GIRLS 1-3
CORRUPTED BY A GANGSTA 1-4
BLINDED BY HIS LOVE
THE PRICE YOU PAY FOR LOVE 1-3
DOPE GIRL MAGIC 1-3
By **Destiny Skai**

WHEN A GOOD GIRL GOES BAD
By **Adrienne**

A KINGPIN'S AMBITION
A KINGPIN'S AMBITION II
I MURDER FOR THE DOUGH
By **Ambitious**

THE COST OF LOYALTY 1-3
By **Kweli**

STEPPERS 3 | KING RIO

A GANGSTER'S REVENGE 1-4
THE BOSS MAN'S DAUGHTERS 1-5
A SAVAGE LOVE 1&2
BAE BELONGS TO ME 1&2
A HUSTLER'S DECEIT 1-3
WHAT BAD BITCHES DO 1-3
SOUL OF A MONSTER 1-3
KILL ZONE
A DOPE BOY'S QUEEN 1-3
TIL DEATH 1-3
IMMA DIE BOUT MINE 1-3
By **Aryanna**

TRUE SAVAGE 1-7
DOPE BOY MAGIC 1-3
MIDNIGHT CARTEL 1-3
CITY OF KINGZ 1&2
NIGHTMARE ON SILENT AVE
THE PLUG OF LIL MEXICO 1&2
CLASSIC CITY
By **Chris Green**

A DOPEBOY'S PRAYER
By **Eddie "Wolf" Lee**

THE KING CARTEL 1-3
By **Frank Gresham**

THESE NIGGAS AIN'T LOYAL 1-3
By **Nikki Tee**

GANGSTA SHYT 1-3
By **CATO**

STEPPERS 3 | KING RIO

THE ULTIMATE BETRAYAL
By **Phoenix**

BOSS'N UP 1-3
By **Royal Nicole**

I LOVE YOU TO DEATH
By **Destiny J**

I RIDE FOR MY HITTA
I STILL RIDE FOR MY HITTA
By **Misty Holt**

LOVE & CHASIN' PAPER
By **Qay Crockett**

TO DIE IN VAIN
SINS OF A HUSTLA
By **ASAD**

BROOKLYN HUSTLAZ
By **Boogsy Morina**

BROOKLYN ON LOCK 1 & 2
By **Sonovia**

GANGSTA CITY
By **Teddy Duke**

A DRUG KING AND HIS DIAMOND 1-3
A DOPEMAN'S RICHES
HER MAN, MINE'S TOO 1&2
CASH MONEY HO'S
THE WIFEY I USED TO BE 1&2
PRETTY GIRLS DO NASTY THINGS
By **Nicole Goosby**

LIPSTICK KILLAH 1-3
CRIME OF PASSION 1-3
FRIEND OR FOE 1-3
By **Mimi**

TRAPHOUSE KING 1-3
KINGPIN KILLAZ 1-3
STREET KINGS 1&2
PAID IN BLOOD 1&2
CARTEL KILLAZ 1-3
DOPE GODS 1&2
By **Hood Rich**

STEADY MOBBN' 1-3
THE STREETS STAINED MY SOUL 1-3
By **Marcellus Allen**

WHO SHOT YA 1-3
SON OF A DOPE FIEND 1-3
HEAVEN GOT A GHETTO 1&2
SKI MASK MONEY 1&2
By **Renta**

GORILLAZ IN THE BAY 1-4
TEARS OF A GANGSTA 1/&2
3X KRAZY 1&2
STRAIGHT BEAST MODE 1&2
By **DE'KARI**

TRIGGADALE 1-3
MURDA WAS THE CASE 1-3
By **Elijah R. Freeman**

THE STREETS ARE CALLING
By **Duquie Wilson**

SLAUGHTER GANG 1-3
RUTHLESS HEART 1-3
By **Willie Slaughter**

GOD BLESS THE TRAPPERS 1-3
THESE SCANDALOUS STREETS 1-3
FEAR MY GANGSTA 1-5
THESE STREETS DON'T LOVE NOBODY 1-2
BURY ME A G 1-5
A GANGSTA'S EMPIRE 1-4
THE DOPEMAN'S BODYGAURD 1&2
THE REALEST KILLAZ 1-3
THE LAST OF THE OGS 1-3
By **Tranay Adams**

MARRIED TO A BOSS 1-3
By **Destiny Skai & Chris Green**

KINGZ OF THE GAME 1-7
CRIME BOSS 1-3
By **Playa Ray**

FUK SHYT
By **Blakk Diamond**

DON'T F#CK WITH MY HEART 1&2
By **Linnea**

ADDICTED TO THE DRAMA 1-3
IN THE ARM OF HIS BOSS
By **Jamila**

LOYALTY AIN'T PROMISED 1&2
By **Keith Williams**

YAYO 1-4
A SHOOTER'S AMBITION 1&2
BRED IN THE GAME
By **S. Allen**

TRAP GOD 1-3
RICH $AVAGE 1-3
MONEY IN THE GRAVE 1-3
CARTEL MONEY
By **Martell Troublesome Bolden**

FOREVER GANGSTA 1&2
GLOCKS ON SATIN SHEETS 1&2
By **Adrian Dulan**

TOE TAGZ 1-4
LEVELS TO THIS SHYT 1&2
IT'S JUST ME AND YOU
By **Ah'Million**

KINGPIN DREAMS 1-3
RAN OFF ON DA PLUG
By **Paper Boi Rari**

CONFESSIONS OF A GANGSTA 1-4
CONFESSIONS OF A JACKBOY 1-3
CONFESSIONS OF A HITMAN
By **Nicholas Lock**

I'M NOTHING WITHOUT HIS LOVE
SINS OF A THUG
TO THE THUG I LOVED BEFORE
A GANGSTA SAVED XMAS
IN A HUSTLER I TRUST
By **Monet Dragun**

QUIET MONEY 1-3
THUG LIFE 1-3
EXTENDED CLIP 1&2
A GANGSTA'S PARADISE
By **Trai'Quan**

CAUGHT UP IN THE LIFE 1-3
THE STREETS NEVER LET GO 1-3
By **Robert Baptiste**

NEW TO THE GAME 1-3
MONEY, MURDER & MEMORIES 1-3
By **Malik D. Rice**

CREAM 2-3
THE STREETS WILL TALK
By **Yolanda Moore**

LIFE OF A SAVAGE 1-4
A GANGSTA'S QUR'AN 1-4
MURDA SEASON 1-3
GANGLAND CARTEL 1-3
CHI'RAQ GANGSTAS 1-4
KILLERS ON ELM STREET 1-3
JACK BOYZ N DA BRONX 1-3
A DOPEBOY'S DREAM 1-3
JACK BOYS VS DOPE BOYS 1-3
COKE GIRLZ
COKE BOYS
SOSA GANG 1&2
BRONX SAVAGES
BODYMORE KINGPINS
BLOOD OF A GOON
By **Romell Tukes**

STEPPERS 3 | KING RIO

THE STREETS MADE ME 1-3
By **Larry D. Wright**

CONCRETE KILLA 1-3
VICIOUS LOYALTY 1-3
By **Kingpen**

THE ULTIMATE SACRIFICE 1-6
KHADIFI
IF YOU CROSS ME ONCE 1-3
ANGEL 1-4
IN THE BLINK OF AN EYE
By **Anthony Fields**

THE LIFE OF A HOOD STAR
By **Ca$h & Rashia Wilson**

THE STREETS WILL NEVER CLOSE 1-3
By **K'ajji**

NIGHTMARES OF A HUSTLA 1-3
By **King Dream**

HARD AND RUTHLESS 1&2
MOB TOWN 251
THE BILLIONAIRE BENTLEYS 1-3
REAL G'S MOVE IN SILENCE
By **Von Diesel**

GHOST MOB
By **Stilloan Robinson**

MOB TIES 1-6
SOUL OF A HUSTLER, HEART OF A KILLER 1-3
GORILLAZ IN THE TRENCHES
By **SayNoMore**

BODYMORE MURDERLAND 1-3
THE BIRTH OF A GANGSTER 1-4
By **Delmont Player**

FOR THE LOVE OF A BOSS 1&2
By **C. D. Blue**

KILLA KOUNTY 1-5
By **Khufu**

MOBBED UP 1-4
THE BRICK MAN 1-5
THE COCAINE PRINCESS 1-10
STEPPERS 1-3
SUPER GREMLIN 1-4
By **King Rio**

MONEY GAME 1&2
By **Smoove Dolla**

A GANGSTA'S KARMA 1-4
By **FLAME**

KING OF THE TRENCHES 1-3
By **GHOST & TRANAY ADAMS**

QUEEN OF THE ZOO 1&2
By **Black Migo**

GRIMEY WAYS 1-3
By **Ray Vinci**

XMAS WITH AN ATL SHOOTER
By **Ca$h & Destiny Skai**

STEPPERS 3 | KING RIO

KING KILLA 1&2
By **Vincent "Vitto" Holloway**

BETRAYAL OF A THUG 1&2
By **Fre$h**

THE MURDER QUEENS 1-5
By **Michael Gallon**

FOR THE LOVE OF BLOOD 1-4
By **Jamel Mitchell**

HOOD CONSIGLIERE 1&2
NO TIME FOR ERROR
By **Keese**

PROTÉGÉ OF A LEGEND 1&2
LOVE IN THE TRENCHES 1&2
By **Corey Robinson**

BORN IN THE GRAVE 1-3
CRIME PAYS
By **Self Made Tay**

MOAN IN MY MOUTH
By **XTASY**

TORN BETWEEN A GANGSTER AND A GENTLEMAN
By **J-BLUNT & Miss Kim**

LOYALTY IS EVERYTHING 1-3
CITY OF SMOKE 1&2
By **Molotti**

HERE TODAY GONE TOMORROW 1&2
By **Fly Rock**

WOMEN LIE MEN LIE 1-4
FIFTY SHADES OF SNOW 1-3
STACK BEFORE YOU SPLURGE
GIRLS FALL LIKE DOMINOES
NAÏVE TO THE STREETS
By **ROY MILLIGAN**

PILLOW PRINCESS
By **S. Hawkins**

THE BUTTERFLY MAFIA 1-3
SALUTE MY SAVAGERY 1&2
By **Fumiya Payne**

THE LANE 1&2
By Ken-Ken Spence

THE PUSSY TRAP 1-5
By **Nene Capri**

DIRTY DNA
By **Blaque**

SANCTIFIED AND HORNY
by **XTASY**

BOOKS BY LDP'S CEO, CA$H

TRUST IN NO MAN
TRUST IN NO MAN 2
TRUST IN NO MAN 3
BONDED BY BLOOD
SHORTY GOT A THUG
THUGS CRY
THUGS CRY 2
THUGS CRY 3
TRUST NO BITCH
TRUST NO BITCH 2
TRUST NO BITCH 3
TIL MY CASKET DROPS
RESTRAINING ORDER
RESTRAINING ORDER 2
IN LOVE WITH A CONVICT
LIFE OF A HOOD STAR
XMAS WITH AN ATL SHOOTER

www.ingramcontent.com/pod-product-compliance
Lightning Source LLC
Chambersburg PA
CBHW071203260626
47162CB00003B/1148